Lane's End

A Fitzjohn Mystery

JILL PATERSON

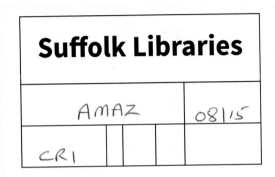
Lane's End

Copyright © 2014 Jill Paterson

This is a work of fiction. Names, characters, places and incidents either are the product of the author's imagination or are used fictitiously, and any resemblance to any actual persons, living or dead, events, or locales is entirely coincidental.

ISBN 978-0-9873955-9-7

Publisher: J. Henderson, Canberra, Australia

Cover design by Renee Barratt
http://www.thecovercounts.com

Also by Jill Paterson

The Celtic Dagger
Murder At The Rocks
Once Upon A Lie

For Brandon

ACKNOWLEDGEMENTS

My gratitude goes to Toner Stevenson, Manager of the Sydney Observatory for giving her permission for the Observatory's image to be used for the cover of Lane's End. My appreciation also goes to, Nicola Begotti, of Pasotti Ombrelli SRL, for giving me his permission to use the, Pasotti, image of the silver cane on the cover. Thank you also to my dear friend and editor, Catherine Hammond, for her much valued expertise, and to Greg Bastian for the proofreading. Last but by no means least, thank you to Melissa McMaugh, Anna Mullins and Malla Duncan for their support throughout the writing process.

Lane's End

☞ CHAPTER 1 ☜

With his wire-framed glasses balanced on the bridge of his nose, Alistair Fitzjohn hummed to himself as he turned the key in the lock and stepped into his sandstone cottage in Birchgrove. Relishing his success at winning North Shore Orchid Society's, 'Orchid of the Evening', he beamed at the prize-winning specimen.

'Who would have thought you'd be my first win?' he said.

With both hands now clasped around the precious object's purple pot, he closed the front door with his foot and made his way through the house to the kitchen before stepping out into the back garden. There, a warm evening breeze ruffled the few wisps of hair that remained on the top of Fitzjohn's head while his gaze took in the flowerbeds, their fragrances wafting in the air around him. At the bottom of the garden stood the new Victorian greenhouse, its shape bathed in moonlight. Sophie had been right, he thought to himself as he made his way down the stone path; it is the Rolls Royce of greenhouses. Edith would love it. A hint of sadness tinged Fitzjohn's thoughts as his late wife's smile came to mind.

Sighing, and balancing the orchid's pot in one hand, he unlatched the greenhouse glass door and stepped into its warm, humid atmosphere. Once inside, he placed the prize-winner in pride of place at the end of the centre bench and stood back to admire it against the rows of other orchids, their delicate blooms wax-like in the soft light. To add to this peaceful scene, Fitzjohn turned to switch on the CD player that sat on the shelf next to the door but as he did so, a soft tap sounded. Peering through the glass, he could see the tall, slim, figure of his young, ginger-haired sergeant, Martin Betts.

Fitzjohn groaned and opened the door. 'Betts? Why do I have the distinct feeling that you're about to spoil my evening?'

Betts, his tall frame towering over Fitzjohn, cleared his throat. 'I apologise, sir, but we've been called out to attend a homicide.'

Fitzjohn's shoulders sagged and he turned to close the greenhouse door, his gaze falling upon the rows of orchids standing like shadowy sentinels, waiting for his return.

'Okay, whereabouts is this homicide?' he asked, making his way back along the garden path.

'Observatory Hill, sir.'

Mumbling to himself, Fitzjohn opened the back door of the house and marched inside.

'You know, Betts, I had the most stupendous evening planned. Do you know why?'

'No, sir,' replied Betts, following Fitzjohn into the kitchen.

'Well, I'll tell you. Tonight I won 'Orchid of the Evening' with my Paphiopedilum woluwense.'

'That's great, sir. Really great.'

'It's not just great, Betts. It's *remarkable!*'

Fitzjohn removed his glasses and commenced to clean them with his handkerchief. 'I've been trying to win that prize for the past two years, and I was planning to have a glass or two of that whisky over there to celebrate.' Fitzjohn looked longingly at a bottle of Glenfiddich that sat on the kitchen table.

'Sorry about that, sir.'

'So am I, Betts. *So* am I.'

With a sigh, Fitzjohn grabbed his briefcase from the kitchen table and, followed by his sergeant, headed for the front door and out to the waiting car.

'Fill me in,' he continued as he settled himself into the passenger seat before pulling the seat belt across his recently acquired trim shape.

Betts slid into the driver's seat. 'All I know at this stage is that the victim was found in the grounds of the Observatory about an hour and a half ago. Apparently a guest at a function being held there this evening.'

'Male or female?'

'Middle-aged male, sir.'

Nearing midnight, they drove in silence as their car sped over Anzac Bridge, the lights from the bridge and Sydney's CBD shimmering in the waters of the harbour. Fitzjohn's thoughts returned to his greenhouse and the haven it provided from scenes such as the one he was about to observe. Betts's eyes remained on the road as he maneuvered the car through the back streets of the city before turning onto Watson Road where they ascended Observatory Hill. At the top, he pulled over in front of the Observatory's tall wrought iron gates where a young constable stood.

'Good evening, sir,' he said to Fitzjohn, his air of enthusiasm tinged with tension, reminding Fitzjohn of his own early days in the North Yorkshire Police.

'Evening, Constable,' replied Fitzjohn.

'You'll find the victim at the rear of the Observatory, sir, behind a marquee.'

'Thank you.'

Fitzjohn and Betts ducked under the police tape and continued on through the open gates, their shoes crunching in the gravel under foot. The edifice of the old Observatory building loomed ahead, its shape casting a shadow across the grounds. In silence, they made their way along the side of the building to the rear corner where a white marquee came into view and not far behind it, a blue forensic tent. While Betts continued on to the marquee, Fitzjohn approached the entrance to the tent. There he found the tall, thin figure of the pathologist, Charles Conroy, along with the SOCO's who worked silently around him. The victim lay on his side at Conroy's feet.

'Charles. Good to see you,' said Fitzjohn, his eye catching sight of the victim's left arm twisted into an impossible position beneath his torso, his right arm stretched out before him. Fitzjohn shivered. Thirty years of such scenes, and still it shocked his system. 'What do we have?' he asked as he crouched down.

'A male, probably in his mid-fifties.'

Conroy joined Fitzjohn beside the body. 'As you can see, not a large man. In fact, he looks rather frail. He's suffered blunt force trauma to the right temple as well as a little further back across the side of the head. I'd say it caused a subdural haematoma which basically means the force of the blow was transferred throughout his skull.'

'Do we have a murder weapon?' asked Fitzjohn, peering closer at the victim's wound.

'I believe it's that walking cane, Alistair.' Conroy pointed to where the SOCO's gathered. The cane lay adjacent to the victim's body, whose right-hand middle finger could be seen barely touching the cane's silver handle; that of an eagle's head.

'It almost looks as though he was reaching for it,' said Fitzjohn. 'Do you have any idea what time he died, Charles?'

'At this stage I'd say he's been dead for about two and a half hours.'

'So, around 9:30pm,' said Fitzjohn, getting to his feet.

'Roughly, yes. I'll be able to give you a more precise time after the post mortem.'

As Charles Conroy spoke, Betts appeared at the tent opening.

'Ah, Betts,' said Fitzjohn. 'How did you get on?'

'A woman by the name of Amanda Marsh found the body at around ten, sir, after most of the other guests had departed.'

'Right.' Fitzjohn turned back to the pathologist. 'No doubt I'll see you later today, Charles.'

'So, who else other than Amanda Marsh is still here?' asked Fitzjohn as he and Betts left the tent.

Betts looked at his notebook. 'There's Emerson Hunt, one of the hosts of the cocktail party, his wife Theodora Hunt, and a man by the name of Sebastian Newberry, sir. They're waiting in the marquee.'

'You said one of the hosts. How many were there at the beginning of the evening?'

'Two. The other, a gentleman by the name of Richard Carmichael, became ill and left around nine o'clock, accompanied by his wife, Laura Carmichael.'

'Very well, I'll speak to Ms Marsh first. Where is she? In the marquee with the others?'

'No, sir. She's over there.' Betts pointed to a woman who stood at the wrought iron railings that overlooked Sydney Harbour. 'Her company catered for the function this evening.'

Fitzjohn followed Betts's gaze to the tall, willowy, figure, her light green dress blowing softly in the evening breeze.

'While I speak to her, Betts, try and scrounge up the function's guest list.'

As Betts disappeared back into the marquee, Fitzjohn made his way across to where the caterer stood.

'Ms Marsh?'

On hearing her name, the woman turned to face Fitzjohn, her silver grey hair cut short and sharp, accentuating high cheekbones and almond shaped eyes. 'Yes?' she replied in a low soft voice.

'I'm Detective Chief Inspector Fitzjohn. I understand that you found the gentleman who died here this evening.'

'That's right.' Amanda Marsh's voice quavered. Noting this, Fitzjohn gestured through a lattice gateway toward a wooden bench near the Observatory's side entrance. 'Why don't we take a seat over there?'

Amanda stumbled as they reached the bench.

'I know this is difficult,' said Fitzjohn as he sat down next to her. 'But there are questions I must ask.'

'I understand completely.' Amanda cleared her throat. 'I'll be fine. It's all been a bit of a shock, that's all,' she said, stemming a tear with her tissue.

'It's a confronting experience.' Fitzjohn paused for a moment before he continued. 'I understand that your company catered for the function this evening. Is that correct?'

'Yes. I don't usually attend, but we're short-staffed at the moment, so I came along to make sure everything went smoothly. I was making a final sweep of the grounds, picking up glasses and plates left outside the marquee, when I tripped on something in the dark. When I looked down I saw the man lying there.' Amanda swallowed hard and looked toward the blue forensic tent, illuminated in the darkness.

'Did you see anyone else in the grounds at the time?'

'No. Everyone had left by then except for Mr and Mrs Hunt and Mr Newberry. They were inside the marquee. They ran out when I screamed. Mr Newberry took charge straight away. He was very good. He tried to find a pulse on the man's neck. While he was doing that, Mr Hunt called triple zero. Then we waited.'

'Did you all stay at the scene?'

'I think so.' Amanda shook her head. 'To tell you the truth, I can't remember.'

'Well, not surprising under the circumstances,' replied Fitzjohn. 'Do you recall seeing the man who died during the course of the evening?'

'Yes. He was one of the first guests to arrive. I offered him a drink, but he declined.'

'Did you notice who he spoke to by any chance?'

'Not really. I was too busy.' Amanda paused. 'I'm sorry, Chief Inspector. I'm not much help.'

'Even the smallest piece of information is important in a case such as this, Ms Marsh. It enables us to form a picture.' Fitzjohn smiled and got to his feet. 'We'll leave it there for now although I might need to speak to you again at some stage. Are you all right to drive? If not, I can arrange transport for you.'

'I think I can manage,' said Amanda. 'I live in Glebe, so I haven't got far to go. I gave the sergeant my address earlier.'

As Amanda Marsh made her way from the premises, Fitzjohn turned to see Betts walking toward him. 'Is that the guest list?' he asked, peering at the sheet of paper in Betts's hand.

'Yes, sir, and interestingly, the victim's name isn't on it.'

'Is that so?' replied Fitzjohn as they walked toward the marquee. 'Perhaps the remaining host can tell us why.'

They reached the entrance to the marquee to find a man of medium height with fine features and a long sharp nose, smoking a cigarette. He threw the cigarette to the ground and squashed it with the sole of his shoe when he saw the two police officers approaching.

'Good evening, sir. I'm DCI Fitzjohn. I believe you've met DS Betts.'

'Yes, I have. I'm Sebastian Newberry. Mr and Mrs Hunt are inside.'

Newberry led the way into the marquee where another man in his mid-fifties with short curly hair tinged with grey, paced the floor. A woman, her plump shape squeezed into a brightly coloured floral dress, sat at one of the tables.

'Mr and Mrs Hunt?' asked Fitzjohn.

The man stopped pacing while the woman turned in her chair to face the two officers.

'Yes. I'm Emerson Hunt,' said the man. 'And this is my wife, Theodora.'

'I'm Detective Chief Inspector Fitzjohn. Considering the hour, I'll try to be brief, but I know you will all appreciate the necessity to get the facts while things are still fresh in your minds.' Fitzjohn gestured to the table where Theodora Hunt sat. When they were all seated, he continued. 'Before we start, I should inform you that we're treating this as a suspicious death.'

'You mean the man was murdered?' said Theodora, her voice but a whisper. 'He didn't just fall over and hit his head?'

'It doesn't appear so, Mrs Hunt, although it does remain to be determined at the post mortem,' replied Fitzjohn, sitting down. 'Now, might I start with you, Mr Hunt? I understand that this evening's cocktail party was hosted by yourself and your business partner, Richard Carmichael.'

Emerson Hunt cleared his throat. 'Yes, that's right. Carmichael Hunt Real Estate is the name of our company. I daresay you've heard of us. We have offices throughout New

South Wales and Victoria.' Hunt's eyes went from Fitzjohn to Betts and back. When no response came from either man, he continued. 'This evening's function was held specifically for some of Richard's and my long-standing clients. Except, of course, for Sebastian, who is Richard's half-brother. But you probably already know that.'

'No we didn't,' replied Fitzjohn, turning to Newberry, who sat thoughtfully stroking his goatee. 'Are you in the real estate business too, Mr Newberry?'

'No, I'm an interior designer. The reason I came along this evening is because many of Richard and Emerson's clients are also my clients.'

'I see. Your brother and his wife left early, I understand.'

'Yes. Richard wasn't feeling well.'

'Exactly what time did they leave?'

'It was just after nine,' put in Theodora.

Fitzjohn looked to both Emerson and Sebastian, who nodded in agreement before he said, 'Amanda Marsh told me that you were the first person to respond to her call for help, Mr Newberry. Can you tell us your recollection of events?'

'Yes, of course.' Newberry stubbed his cigarette out in the ashtray and sat up straight in his chair. 'It was around ten o'clock when I heard the scream. I remember because I was just about to leave. Anyway, I ran straight out of the marquee and found Amanda standing over the man. At first I thought he'd had too much to drink and fallen, but when I saw the cut on the side of his head, I realised he was hurt quite badly. That's when I tried to find a pulse but, regrettably, he was already gone.'

'Did anyone leave the scene before the police arrived?' asked Fitzjohn.

'I ran back to the marquee to get my coat,' replied Theodora. 'To put over the man. I thought he might be in shock. I didn't realise he was... dead.'

'What about Amanda Marsh?'

'Oh, well, she was inconsolable,' said Emerson. 'As soon as the police arrived, I took her into the marquee and gave her a shot of brandy.'

Fitzjohn looked to each of those seated. 'Very well. Now, according to the victim's identification, his name was Peter Van Goren. Was he one of your clients, Mr Hunt, or one of Richard Carmichael's?'

'He wasn't one of mine, so he must have been Richard's.'

'I don't remember seeing the name Peter Van Goren on the guest list,' remarked Theodora.

'That's because it isn't there, Mrs Hunt,' said Fitzjohn.

'Mmm. That's typical,' put in Emerson. 'Richard must have omitted to include him on the list.' He looked to Fitzjohn. 'Unfortunately, my business partner can be a bit slap dash, at times, Chief Inspector.'

'So,' continued Fitzjohn. 'Am I to understand that none of you knew the deceased? What about you, Mr Newberry? Is the name Peter Van Goren familiar?'

'No, it isn't. I've never heard the name before.'

'Do you remember speaking to Mr Van Goren during the course of the evening?'

'No.'

Fitzjohn turned to the Hunts. 'And you, Mrs Hunt. Did you speak to Peter Van Goren?'

'I greeted him when he first arrived. And you had a word with him too, didn't you, darling?' she said, looking towards her husband.

'Briefly. Yes. Early on in the evening.' Emerson struck a match and lit a cigarette, drawing the smoke into his lungs.

'Did any of you happen to see who else he spoke to?'

Emerson sat back and watched the smoke from his cigarette curl in the air around him. 'I was too busy seeing to my clients to notice.'

'I saw him speak to Richard,' said Theodora. 'And if I'm not mistaken, they were arguing.' Emerson shot a look at his wife and his eyes narrowed.

'Do you have any idea what they were arguing about, Mrs Hunt?' asked Fitzjohn with growing interest.

'Not really, although I did hear Ben's name mentioned. That's Richard's son. And I also heard Richard tell the man to leave at once.' Theodora Hunt caught her husband's intense stare.

The look was not lost on Fitzjohn. 'Very well,' he said, looking at his watch before getting to his feet. 'We'll leave it there for now, but I do ask that you keep yourselves available because I'm sure there'll be more questions as the day progresses.'

A chill filled the night air as Fitzjohn and Betts made their way back through the Observatory grounds to the car.

'So, the victim died at approximately nine-thirty and according to the Hunts and Newberry, Richard Carmichael and his wife left the cocktail party just after nine,' said Fitzjohn.

'That eliminates the Carmichaels then, sir.'

'Not necessarily, Betts. After all, it depends on how long it took Peter Van Goren to die. He could have been lying out there in the grounds for some time before death occurred. Anyway, we'll know for sure after the post mortem.' Fitzjohn undid the button on his suit coat and climbed into the passenger seat.

'Emerson Hunt didn't look pleased when his wife told us that Richard Carmichael had argued with the victim, sir,' continued Betts, starting the car.

'No. I dare say Mr Hunt wants to protect his partner at all costs. Being a person of interest in such a crime can't be good for business. Of course they all are. Persons of interest, that is.' Fitzjohn paused. 'I wonder if Richard Carmichael's sudden attack of ill health was conveniently orchestrated. When you think about it, if he did kill Peter Van Goren, the best place to be is anywhere but at the murder scene. If only we knew what they argued about.' Fitzjohn fell silent before he continued. 'Of course, Emerson Hunt might be able to answer that question because he's hiding something.'

'He is?'

'Most certainly. I feel it in my bones.'

'All I feel in my bones right now is a night's sleep coming on.'

Fitzjohn looked over at his young sergeant. 'There's no point in even thinking about it, Betts, because it's not going to happen. We need to make contact with the victim's next-of-kin as soon as possible.'

'But it's two in the morning, sir,' replied Betts with a groan.

'I don't care what time it is. Mr Van Goren's relatives need to know what's happened to him. Where did he live?'

'Vaucluse, sir.'

'Then we'll make our way there now.'

☞ CHAPTER 2 ☜

In the early hours of Saturday morning, Wentworth Avenue in Vaucluse lay deserted. Betts pulled up in front of Peter Van Goren's home.

'This is it, sir. Shall I drive in?'

Fitzjohn peered out of the passenger car window at a wide sweeping circular driveway that meandered through a leafy garden and beneath a portico at the front door of the residence before emerging once again onto the street.

'No. I think we'll cause enough disruption without the car pulling up too.' Fitzjohn climbed out and looked thoughtfully toward the house partly shrouded behind trees and bushes, themselves only shadows in the darkness. 'Why does the task of telling people of their loved ones demise feel worse in the dead of the night?'

Together they made their way, reluctantly, to the front door. Betts rang the bell while Fitzjohn straightened his suit coat and adjusted his tie. After a few minutes, the heavy oak door opened to reveal a woman in her early sixties clasping her long blue dressing gown around herself. Barely visible through the wrought iron security door, she looked guardedly at the two men.

'Good morning, madam,' said Fitzjohn. 'I'm Detective Chief Inspector Fitzjohn. This is Detective Sergeant Betts. We're from the New South Wales Police Force.' The woman narrowed her eyes at their warrant cards before peering again at Fitzjohn and Betts. 'I apologise for the early hour. May we speak to Mrs Van Goren?'

'There isn't a Mrs Van Goren,' said the woman in a soft voice.

'I see,' replied Fitzjohn. 'Then can you tell us where we can find Mr Van Goren's next-of-kin?'

'As far as I know, he doesn't have any, Chief Inspector. I'm Ida Clegg, Mr Van Goren's housekeeper. Has something happened to him?'

'I'm afraid so, Mrs Clegg. Might we come inside?'

'I'd prefer you didn't. Especially at this time of night. Let's face it, you could be anybody.'

'I can appreciate your hesitation, Mrs Clegg. The reason for our call is that Mr Van Goren's body was found earlier this evening at the Observatory where he'd been attending a cocktail party.'

'Oh.' Ida Clegg wavered, her hand catching onto the large knob in the centre of the front door. 'On second thought, perhaps you'd better come in because I have to sit down.'

Ida unlatched the security door. 'Come through,' she said, running her left arm along the wall for support as she led the way into a large living room. 'We can talk in here,' she said, falling into an armchair. 'You said Mr Van Goren's body was found. That means he's dead.'

'Yes,' replied Fitzjohn.

The palm of Ida Clegg's hand went across her mouth. 'How?' she whispered. 'Did he have a fall? He wasn't too steady on his feet, you know.'

Fitzjohn and Betts settled themselves onto the sofa. 'He did fall, but it wasn't through his own imbalance,' replied Fitzjohn. 'I'm afraid we're treating Mr Van Goren's death as suspicious.'

Ida Clegg winced. 'You mean someone killed him?'

'That's yet to be determined, but it does look to be the case.'

Tears brimmed Ida's eyes and she fumbled in her dressing gown pocket before bringing out a small embroidered handkerchief to dab her eyes. 'But why would anyone want to hurt Mr Van Goren? I don't understand. I really don't.'

Fitzjohn waited for a few moments before he said, 'How long have you worked for Mr Van Goren?'

'Oh, a long time. I started in 1986, just after he moved into this house. He told me he'd bought the place because of its location on the edge of the harbour. What he hadn't considered was its size. Anyway, that's why he decided he needed a housekeeper.' Ida blinked back tears.

'Are you his only employee?'

'No. There's also Marge, the cook, although she's not here at the moment. She went to stay with her sister in Wollongong for the weekend. And there's Len. He's the grounds man. He has a small apartment out there in the garden.' Ida gestured to the plate glass window where their images could be seen reflected against the inky blackness outside.

'You mentioned that Mr Van Goren wasn't always steady on his feet,' continued Fitzjohn.

'No, he wasn't. There was something wrong with his right leg. He always walked with a cane. At least he has since I've known him.' Mrs Clegg sighed. 'I don't know what was wrong with his leg. He didn't offer to tell me and I would never have asked. He was a very private man, you see.'

'Can you describe his walking cane?'

Mrs Clegg gave Fitzjohn a quizzical look. 'Well, he has several, but the one he took with him when he left the house on Friday afternoon, was made of rosewood and has a silver handle in the shape of an eagle's head. There's also a silver tip on the end, although that's covered up with a piece of rubber to prevent the silver being damaged. It was his favourite. Mr Van Goren once told me that it had belonged to his father.'

'You said earlier that you don't think Mr Van Goren has any next-of-kin.'

'That's because in all the years I've known him, he's never had contact with any relatives to my knowledge. At least none have ever called here.' Ida Clegg paused. 'Still, I don't suppose that means there aren't any. Come to think of it, they might live overseas. He spoke with a slight accent, you see. I thought he could have been Dutch with a name like Van Goren.'

'Do you have any idea how old he was?'

Mrs Clegg's face brightened. 'Well, that question I can answer. He was fifty-nine last birthday.' Ida smiled as if recalling the event. 'Marge, Len and I had a little get-together for him. Marge baked him a sponge cake complete with candles.'

'Did he receive birthday greetings from anyone else?'

'Not that I know of. The only phone call I'm aware he received that day was from his solicitor, Raymond West. It was about one of Mr Van Goren's business interests.'

'Oh? What did Mr Van Goren do for a living?' asked Fitzjohn, looking around the room, its opulence apparent.

'Well, he was a bit of an entrepreneur and although I don't know the extent of his business interests, I do know that he traded on the stock market and also that he owned a number of commercial properties as well as a chain of coffee shops. Other than that, however, I think you'll have to talk to Mr West. I'm sure he'll be able to help you.'

'We'll do that, Mrs Clegg,' replied Fitzjohn. 'Now, I don't want to keep you too much longer but Mr Van Goren arrived at the Observatory last evening in a taxi so I take it he didn't drive.'

'No. He found it difficult with his leg the way it was. He does have a car though. Len used to drive him wherever he wanted to go but on Friday, for some reason, he said he was going by taxi. I offered to order one for him but he said he'd already done so.'

'What taxi company picked him up?'

'It was a Silver Service taxi cab. It arrived at two o'clock on the dot.'

'Did he say where he was going?'

'No.'

'And is that the last time you saw him?'

'Yes, it was.' Mrs Clegg stemmed a tear with her handkerchief.

———————

'You can't help but feel sorry for Mrs Clegg,' said Betts as he and Fitzjohn left the house. 'Her life has changed with no warning after years of loyal service.'

'Mmm. It makes you realise there's no guarantees, doesn't it,' replied Fitzjohn, looking back through the trees. 'Change can come when you least expect it.'

Betts unlocked the car doors and they climbed in. 'Where to now, sir?'

'The station. I want the investigative team to meet before day break. After that, I want you to find out where we can speak to Raymond West on a Saturday. Hopefully, he'll be able to fill in some of the blanks concerning Peter Van Goren.'

———————

Fitzjohn adjusted his glasses as he stood at the head of the Incident Room in front of a whiteboard. Gathered before him was an array of plain clothed as well as uniformed police officers. 'Okay everyone,' he said, his voice rising above the din. 'I know it's 4am and we're all tired, but I want to go through what we have so far.' A hush fell over the room. 'Our victim is a fifty-nine year old male, identified as Peter Van Goren. His body was found earlier this evening at approximately ten o'clock in the grounds of the Observatory whilst he was attending a cocktail party.' Fitzjohn lowered his glasses along the bridge of his nose and looked over them as he turned to point to a photograph of Van Goren's body on the whiteboard. 'As you're by now aware, the victim suffered two blows to the right side of the head. However, it's still to be determined whether these injuries were the cause of death. As far as physical evidence of the attack is concerned, this silver handled cane was recovered from the scene.' Fitzjohn pointed to a second, enlarged, photograph showing the intricate silver carving of an eagle's head. A stir went through the room.

Fitzjohn continued. 'The function was hosted by business partners, Richard Carmichael and Emerson Hunt, and attended by eighty-three guests. It should be noted that our victim was not included amongst those invited. Guests started to leave the function at approximately nine-thirty. Nine-thirty is also the estimated time of the victim's death.'

'What about next-of-kin, sir?' asked a young female police officer, sitting at a desk at the front of the room. 'As yet, we haven't been able to make contact with Mr Van Goren's next-of-kin.'

Fitzjohn paused to push his glasses back up over the bridge of his nose. 'That's all we have at this point until such time as forensics have made their conclusions and the post mortem is complete. Our task for now is to interview each and every guest who attended last night's cocktail party, conduct alibi follow-ups and look at phone records. I want your findings on my desk by four o'clock this afternoon.' Another stir went through the crowd as those gathered dispersed.

When the room had emptied, Fitzjohn turned to Betts. 'I want to speak to Mr and Mrs Carmichael as soon as possible.

After that, we'll have another word with the Hunts and that solicitor fellow, Raymond West.' He gave Betts a wry smile. 'Should keep us busy for the day. But, for now,' he added, grabbing his suit coat and shrugging it on, 'I'm going home to change. I suggest you do the same.'

☞ CHAPTER 3 ☜

Fitzjohn looked out of the passenger window and sighed as Betts brought the car to a stand-still outside the Carmichael's home on Prince Albert Street in Mosman. 'It seems the gods aren't looking favourably on us this morning.'

Betts followed Fitzjohn's gaze up the winding steps through a tiered, manicured garden that led to the imposing residence high above the roadway. When they reached the front door, Fitzjohn took his handkerchief from the breast pocket of his suit coat and wiped his brow while Betts rang the bell. The door opened almost at once and a young woman in her mid-twenties appeared. She was dressed in a pair of blue jeans and a loose fitting light grey top that gave her a breezy air, but belied the tension evident across her face.

'Can I help you?' she asked, a wary look in her dark blue eyes.

The two officers introduced themselves and held up their warrant cards. 'We're here to speak to Mr and Mrs

Carmichael,' replied Fitzjohn. 'It's in relation to a function they hosted at the Sydney Observatory on Friday evening.'

'I'm sorry, they're not here, Chief Inspector.'

'Oh? When will they be back, Ms..?'

'It's Carmichael. Joanna Carmichael. I don't know when my parents will be back.'

With trembling hands the young woman pushed the wisps of fair hair framing her face back into her pony tail. 'You see, my father suffered a heart attack through the night. He's been taken to North Shore Hospital.'

'I'm sorry to hear that,' replied Fitzjohn, taken aback.

'It's about the person who died at the Observatory last night, isn't it? My step-mother, Laura, expected you might call round. She asked me to tell you that she's more than willing to speak to you, but it'll have to be at the hospital. She won't leave my father's bedside at a time like this.'

'Of course. Look, I think under the circumstances, we'll make it another time, Ms Carmichael. Can you let her know, please?'

'Yes, of course.' Fitzjohn and Betts turned to leave. 'I don't suppose I can help you with your enquiries, can I?'

'Not unless you were at the cocktail party last night and I don't remember seeing your name on the guest list,' replied Fitzjohn, turning back.

'Well, that's just it. I was there, albeit, for a short period of time.' Joanna stepped back from the door. 'Come through to the sun-room. We can talk there.' Fitzjohn and Betts followed Joanna through the house to a large living area, its floor-to-ceiling glass windows overlooking a garden shaded by tall trees and filled with blooms of every variety. She gestured to the sofas and chairs, each with billowing cushions, grouped around a glass-topped coffee table. 'Please, have a seat.'

Fitzjohn sank into an armchair, the cushions consuming him. Betts shot an amused look his way before he sat down himself on one of the sofas and opened his notebook.

'It's a very comfortable room, Ms Carmichael, and the garden looks remarkable,' Fitzjohn commented.

Joanna looked around wistfully. 'Needless to say, it's my father's favourite room in the house. He sits here and watches Laura toil in the garden. Of course, it's her passion. She has what they call a green thumb.' Joanna sighed and looked back at Fitzjohn and Betts.

'I hope I can help with your enquiries even though I wasn't at the function for very long. The only reason I went was to drop off some papers that Dad forgot to take with him.' Joanna caught Fitzjohn's questioning look. 'I work in the Carmichael Hunt Real Estate office.'

'Oh, I see. What time did you arrive at the cocktail party, Ms Carmichael?' asked Fitzjohn.

'About seven-thirty. The thing is, Chief Inspector, I think I might have spoken to the man who died. I heard on the news this morning that he walked with a cane.'

'That's right. It has a silver handle in the shape of an eagle's head,' replied Fitzjohn.

'Well, in that case, I did speak to him. We arrived at the Observatory at the same time, and we spoke as we walked through the grounds to the marquee.' Joanna Carmichael paused. 'I think he said his name was Peter. I can't remember his surname.'

'It's was Van Goren.'

'Ah, yes, that was it. I knew it was something unusual.'

'What did you speak to Mr Van Goren about?' continued Fitzjohn.

'The weather to start with and then he asked how my brother, Ben, was and whether he'd be there that evening. He seemed disappointed when I told him he wouldn't be. I guess he must have known Ben. Seems a bit odd really. I thought I knew all my brother's friends,' she added as if to herself.

'Was there any reason Mr Van Goren should have expected your brother to be there?'

'I can't think of one. Ben never attends the company's functions. He has no reason to. He's not involved in the business.' Joanna fell silent before she added, 'It's going to be such a shock for him when he hears what's happened to our Dad.'

'He doesn't know?' asked Fitzjohn.

'No. He's been overseas for the past few weeks. He's a photojournalist. Spends most of his time in the world's trouble spots. He arrives back home tonight.' Joanna paused. 'I tried to phone him last night when Dad was taken to hospital, but his phone was turned off. I guess he'd already boarded his flight.'

'Did you notice who else Peter Van Goren spoke to, by any chance?' asked Fitzjohn.

Joanna thought for a moment. 'I seem to remember he had a word with Theodora. She's the wife of my father's business partner, Emerson Hunt.'

'Was there anyone else?'

'I don't know. We got separated after that.' Joanna met Fitzjohn's gaze. 'I hope you don't think my father had anything to do with this man's death, Chief Inspector. You see, I am aware that he argued with the man who died. Laura told me. She's worried what you might assume. Especially now that Dad isn't able to speak for himself.'

'I understand your concern, Ms Carmichael, and I'll be honest with you, the very fact that your father argued with the deceased does prompt questions.'

'Are you saying he's a suspect?'

'A person of interest, Ms Carmichael, as is everyone who attended the function.'

'Well, I suppose that's some consolation.'

Fitzjohn ignored Joanna's comment and continued. 'Of course, it would help us if we knew what your father and Peter Van Goren argued about. Does your stepmother have any idea?'

Joanna opened her mouth to speak but hesitated before she said, 'No, she doesn't. Look, I hate to cut this sort, but I feel that I should get back to the hospital. Laura's alone and quite upset.'

'Of course,' replied Fitzjohn, struggling to get out of the chair. 'Oh, there's just one quick thing. Do you remember what cab company Peter Van Goren arrived by?'

'Same as me. Silver Service.'

'I could swear that Joanna Carmichael was about to tell us what her father's argument with Van Goren was about, but thought better of it,' said Fitzjohn as he and Betts made their way back to the car.

'Probably because it would have indicated that he knew the victim, sir.' Betts pulled away from the curb.

'Mmm. You might be right. Anyway, whatever it was, there's definitely more going on here than we're seeing right now. Let's hope we can glean something from Mr and Mrs Hunt. Where do they live?'

'In Seaforth, sir.' Betts turned onto Military Road and headed toward the Spit Bridge. 'Shouldn't take long to get there unless we're held up at the Spit.' As Betts said the words, the car rounded the bend in the road to find the traffic backed up the hill. He slammed his foot on the brake. The car came to a sudden stop. Below, in the distance, a yacht glided slowly past the raised Spit Bridge and into Sydney Harbour.

Thrown forward, Fitzjohn glared at Betts. 'I'd like to get there in one piece, if you don't mind.'

'Sorry, sir.'

Minutes passed. Betts drummed his fingers on top of the steering wheel.

'You're very edgy this morning, Betts. What's wrong with you?'

'We've been up all night, sir. I get this way when I don't get enough sleep.'

'Mmm. Well, I think sleep isn't something we're going to get a lot of over the next few days.' Fitzjohn yawned. 'I'm a bit tired myself, come to think of it.'

As the bridge moved back into place, Betts inched the car forward down the hill and across the Spit. They entered the leafy suburb of Seaforth a few minutes later, driving along Abernethy Street and eyeing the properties that rose high above the roadway.

'If I'm right, Emerson and Theodora Hunt live just along here, at number twenty-seven. There it is there, sir.' Betts pulled over and looked up at the terraced garden and sweeping driveway leading to the house. 'Looks like it pays to be in real estate.'

Fitzjohn peered out of the window. 'I prefer something a little smaller myself and closer to the roadway, like my cottage in Birchgrove.' They climbed out of the car and started up the drive. 'Why does everyone have to live on mountain tops?' mumbled Fitzjohn to himself while ignoring Betts, who stopped mid-way to admire a dark grey BMW, its nose edging its way out of the open garage. Carrying on, he reached the front door and rang the bell. When it sounded, a dog barked, after which the door flew open and Emerson Hunt appeared, a scowl across his face. Wearing a pair of track pants and a T-shirt displaying a large green tick, he struggled with a wriggling mass of long white hair caught under his left arm.

'Good morning, Mr Hunt. I wonder if we might speak to you again.' Fitzjohn glanced behind him to see Betts reach the front porch.

Emerson stepped back from the doorway. 'Yes, of course. For a moment there, I thought you were going to be one of those religious groups trying to save my soul. That's all I need right now. Come through, gentlemen,' he continued, now holding the dog at arm's length. 'I daresay you've heard that Richard is in the hospital.'

'Yes,' replied Fitzjohn. 'It's most unfortunate.'

'It certainly is. Especially at a time like this when it could be construed he had something to do with that man's death last night. Not to mention what harm this whole thing is going to do to our business once word gets out.' Fitzjohn glanced sideways at Betts while Hunt stopped at an open doorway. 'If you'd care to wait in there,' he said, gesturing into a large living room. 'I'll get rid of this damned dog.' With that, Emerson disappeared.

'Sounds like Mr Hunt is more concerned with the business side of things than he is about his partner's life,' said Betts, walking into the room and looking around.

'Takes all kinds, Betts.'

While Fitzjohn studied a painting on the wall above the fireplace, Betts crossed to the window and took in the view overlooking Middle Harbour with the Sydney skyline in the distance. 'It's amazing how some people live. Just look at that view. There's no two ways about it, I should have gone into real estate. I can just see myself living in a place like this. Sitting here on a cold winter's evening in front of a roaring fire, relaxing after a hard day at the office selling houses.'

Fitzjohn glanced at Betts and rolled his eyes. As he did so, Emerson Hunt reappeared.

'Have a seat, gentlemen,' Emerson said, sitting down in an armchair. 'I'm sorry about the dog. It belongs to Theodora.'

'I should have mentioned, Mr Hunt,' said Fitzjohn, settling himself into a chair. 'We'd like to speak to Mrs Hunt as well.'

'Oh, I see. Well, she's not here at the moment. She's at the tennis club. Plays every Saturday morning.' Emerson looked at his watch. 'She should be home soon, though.' As he spoke, a door slammed and hurried footsteps could be heard.

'For god's sake, Emerson,' a woman's voice yelled. 'Why did you lock Tulip in the storeroom? You know it frightens her to be in the dark. Oh!' Dressed in a short white tennis dress and cradling Tulip in her arms, Theodora Hunt gaped at Fitzjohn and Betts. 'I didn't know we had company,' she continued in a softer voice as she peered from beneath the neb of her cap.

'The police want to ask us more questions about last night, darling.'

Theodora edged into the room and chose to sit on a long couch where she crossed her plump legs. Tulip curled up on her lap while Theodora removed her cap and shook out her long curly blonde hair.

When she had settled herself, Fitzjohn said, 'Last night you said that you'd both spoken to the deceased. Can you tell us what was said?'

The Hunts glanced at each other before Theodora said, 'Well, in my case, not much. I remarked on what a lovely evening it was and after that, Mr Van Goren caught sight of Richard and went off to speak to him. I told you last night what happened next, didn't I? They argued.'

Emerson Hunt glared at his wife. Theodora returned the look and shrugged.

'And you, Mr Hunt. Do you recollect what your conversation with Peter Van Goren was about?'

'Yes. I admired the uniqueness of the cane he carried.'

'Was that the extent of your conversation?' asked Fitzjohn.

'Pretty much, because we were interrupted.'

'By whom?'

Emerson hesitated. 'By one of my clients. He wanted to introduce me to his wife.' Hunt looked over at Theodora.

'Theo, why don't you put the dog out in the kitchen while these gentlemen are here?'

'You know I can't do that, darling. Tulip hates to be alone. Don't you sweetie pie,' she said, kissing the dog on the head.

Emerson's eyes narrowed with annoyance.

Fitzjohn turned to Theodora. 'Mrs Hunt. You said that you saw Richard Carmichael argue with Peter Van Goren. Can you tell us what time that would have been?'

'Just after eight o'clock, I think.'

'And how long did their argument last?'

'Five minutes or so. They weren't shouting, you understand. But it was obvious that it wasn't a friendly conversation. In the end, Richard ushered Mr Van Goren out of the marquee. I didn't see him after that.'

'What did Richard Carmichael do after Peter Van Goren left?'

'For some reason, he became angry about the food presentation and said he was going to speak to the caterer, Amanda Marsh.

'And how long was he gone?'

'Fifteen minutes or so. It was when he came back that he became ill and Laura took him home.'

Emerson glared at Theodora.

—————

'Why do I get the feeling that things aren't quite what they seem between those two,' asked Betts as they made their way back down the driveway to the car.

'Because they're not,' replied Fitzjohn. 'I'd say there's a great deal of intolerance between them. Not helped along by Mrs Hunt's openness about Richard Carmichael's argument with the victim and, it seems, his disapproval of the caterer's food preparation.'

'What if Richard Carmichael's disapproval was just an excuse to follow Van Goren outside, sir? Perhaps to continue their argument. Things got out of hand and... Van Goren ended up dead.'

'Sounds plausible,' replied Fitzjohn. 'Except for one thing. Theodora Hunt told us that Carmichael left the cocktail party just after nine o'clock. He'd have been well away if Charles Conroy was right about the time of death of nine-thirty. Let's make our way to the morgue and find out if he's changed his mind since doing the post mortem.' Fitzjohn climbed into the car and pulled his seat belt on. 'After that, I want you to find out as much as you can about Mrs Hunt because I'd like to speak to her again, without her husband present. I might be wrong, but I think the lady likes to gossip and it could work in our favour.'

CHAPTER 4

A distinct antiseptic odor filled the air as Fitzjohn and Betts walked into the Parramatta morgue later that morning. After acknowledging the attendant at the front desk, they made their way along the hallway to find Charles Conroy and his assistant in a long rectangular room, its row of stainless steel tables empty except for one where Peter Van Goren's body lay. Fitzjohn's eye became fastened on the still form while Betts entered the room with a measure of apprehension.

'Ah, there you are Alistair,' said Charles when the two officers appeared. 'I'm glad you're here because I was right about the blows to the side of the victim's head. They did cause a subdural haematoma and were the cause of death. But, I have to say that if it hadn't happened, he'd have been dead in a month or so anyway.'

'Why do you say that?' asked Fitzjohn, walking the full length of the room to Conroy's side.

'Because our victim suffered from pancreatic cancer. Quite advanced. So much so that he'd have had little strength to defend himself against his assailant.'

'In that case, could a woman have been his attacker?' asked Fitzjohn, looking down at Peter Van Goren's emaciated body.

'Undoubtedly. He would have had little strength to resist a man or a woman.'

'And the time of death?' asked Fitzjohn.

'I'm going to stick with what I said at the crime scene, Alistair. Nine-thirty, except that I'm going to add that the victim didn't die immediately. After the attack, I'd say the poor beggar clung to life for anything up to an hour.'

A myriad of thoughts ran through Fitzjohn's head.

Fitzjohn and Betts walked from the morgue. 'Well, that changes things, Betts. Van Goren didn't die immediately, after all, which means it's entirely possible that Richard Carmichael could have been his assailant.'

'But what motive would he have, sir?'

'Good question. In fact, what motive would any of the people we've spoken to, so far, have? Including the women.' Fitzjohn glanced at Betts. 'I think in light of what Charles just said about the victim's ill health, we can't discount them from our list of persons of interest, and that includes Laura Carmichael.' Fitzjohn pulled his seat belt on. 'It's quite a list. The question is, where do we begin?'

Betts started the car. 'What if I try to find out as much as I can about Peter Van Goren, sir? It might lead to something.'

'Good idea, Betts. And also speak to the Silver Service taxi cab company. According to Ida Clegg, he left his home in Vaucluse at two on Friday. We need to know what he was doing in the five and a half hours until he arrived at the Observatory.'

Later that morning, Fitzjohn and Betts took the elevator in the building on Phillip Street that housed Raymond West's office. The doors reopened onto the 2nd level where West's name appeared in gold lettering on a glass door. Fitzjohn peered into the unlit interior of the office. 'Are you sure Mr West said he'd be here on a Saturday, Betts?'

'Yes, sir. Until four this afternoon.'

Betts tapped on the glass door. A moment later the interior lights flickered and a stout man with unruly dark curly hair and tortoise-shell rimmed glasses came into view. Straightening his tie and buttoning his rumpled suit coat around a portly girth, he crossed the reception area and unlocked the door.

'Detective Sergeant Betts?' he asked.

'Yes, Mr West, and this is Detective Chief Inspector Fitzjohn.'

Raymond West looked toward Fitzjohn. 'Pleased to meet you, Chief Inspector. Won't you both come in.' West stood back to let Fitzjohn and Betts inside before promptly locking the door again. 'I've only just arrived myself,' he said.

'I should have turned the lights on when I first walked in. Come this way, gentlemen.'

The two officers followed Raymond West across the reception area and into a small office, its dark wood-panelled walls diffusing any light that emanated from the window overlooking the street. He gestured to two green leather-bound chairs in front of a large walnut desk, itself inlaid with green leather.

'Please, make yourselves comfortable,' he said as Fitzjohn and Betts looked around the room. 'It's like walking into the past, I know, but I can't bring myself to alter a thing. We're a family firm, you see, and this office hasn't changed since my grandfather's time.'

He sat down. 'I understand you're here to ask me about my client, Peter Van Goren,' he continued, adjusting his glasses before clasping his hands together. 'I heard about his death on the news this morning and was saddened. Especially since he wasn't a well man.'

'I take it he spoke to you about his ill health, Mr West,' said Fitzjohn.

'Yes. In fact, he did so yesterday. Apparently, he'd spent the afternoon at St Vincent's Hospital. He suffered from some form of cancer, you see, and unfortunately, while he was at the hospital, they told him that it had spread. That's why he came to see me. He wanted to go over his will.'

'Did he make any changes to it?' asked Fitzjohn.

'Only to bring it up-to-date with his added investment properties. Other than that, it remains as it was executed some years ago. As a matter of fact, it was one of the first instructions I took from Mr Van Goren.' West opened a manila folder that sat on the desk in front of him and took out a long thin envelope. 'I have the revised will here, Chief Inspector. I got it out of safe custody in case you wanted to look it over.'

'Can you tell us who the beneficiaries are?' asked Fitzjohn, watching West remove the will from its envelope.

'Other than bequests to his staff, there's only one beneficiary.' West smoothed the pages flat with his hands before he peered through his bifocals. 'His name is Benjamin Carmichael.'

Fitzjohn's brow furrowed. 'Carmichael?'

'That's right.'

'Can you tell us what relation Ben Carmichael was to Peter Van Goren?'

'He wasn't a blood relation. I know that because Mr Van Goren told me as much. He said he had no next-of-kin. As to what connection he had to Mr Carmichael, that I don't know. Mr Van Goren didn't offer that information, I'm afraid.'

'What does the estate entail?' continued Fitzjohn, feeling a surge of interest at the mention of the Carmichael name.

'It's quite substantial,' replied West, looking at Fitzjohn over his glasses. 'Besides monies, stocks and bonds, Mr Van Goren owned a number of commercial properties, and a chain of coffee shops. There's also his home in Vaucluse. That, however, has been left to a member of Mr Van Goren's staff. His housekeeper, Ida Clegg.'

A slight smile came to Betts's face.

'Even so, all in all, I'd say we're looking at an estate of at least fifty million. Perhaps more.'

'Can I ask when you executed Peter Van Goren's first will, Mr West?' asked Fitzjohn.

'Yes, of course. Now, let me see.' Raymond West rummaged through the manila folder and brought out a sheet of paper which he held up. 'This is a list of instructions I have taken from Mr Van Goren over the years.' West perused the list. 'Mmm. I thought so. The first will was executed on the tenth of October, nineteen eighty-six.' West looked up and gave a quick smile.

'So is that when you first met Mr Van Goren?'

'Yes. At the time, he'd just bought his first commercial property.'

<hr>

A soft rain fell as Fitzjohn and Betts left the building and walked toward their car. 'Finally, Betts, we have a connection between the Carmichaels and Peter Van Goren. Van Goren had to have known the family. One doesn't leave their entire estate to a stranger.'

<hr>

With the long day behind him and darkness falling, Fitzjohn walked into his office and closed the blind before he sat down at his desk. As he did so, the office door flew open and Chief Superintendent Grieg walked into the room.

'What the hell's going on?' he roared. 'Why are you involved in the homicide at the Observatory? And why wasn't I told?'

Knowing nothing irritated Grieg more than his temperate demeanor on such occasions, Fitzjohn dug deep to contain his abhorrence of Grieg. 'I daresay that's because you weren't here at the time, sir. But now that you are, I can tell you all about it.' Fitzjohn gave a wry smile.

'Don't patronise me,' spat Grieg.

'I wouldn't think of it,' continued Fitzjohn. 'Would you care to sit down?'

'No, I wouldn't.'

'Very well. In your absence, the Chief Constable merely asked me to take charge of the investigation. He didn't explain why, but I'm sure if you ask him...'

'I know what you're up to, Fitzjohn, and it won't work.' Grieg's fist came down on top of the metal filing cabinet. The vibration sent the frame containing Edith's photograph crashing to the floor.

Fitzjohn's right hand clenched. His eyes locked onto Grieg. 'I have no idea what you mean,' he replied before leaving his desk to pick the photograph up from amidst shards of glass.

'Of course you do,' hissed Grieg. 'And don't think undermining me is going to get you a promotion. It's more likely to get you fired.'

Fitzjohn watched the door to his office slam behind Grieg. Minutes later the door re-opened and Betts's head appeared. 'Everything all right in here?' he asked.

'Couldn't be better,' replied Fitzjohn, brushing Edith's photograph off and placing it carefully against the pot of pens on his desk.

'Chief Superintendent Grieg's in a foul mood since he got back from leave,' continued Betts, glass crunching under the soles of his shoes as he walked across the room. 'Word has it his wife's left him.'

'Oh? That's not good news.'

Fitzjohn sat down heavily behind his desk, his thoughts going back to the previous year and his chance meeting with Grieg and a woman other than Grieg's wife. Not that he was the least bit interested in Grieg's personal life, but the encounter was enough to ensure that Grieg stepped carefully in his dealings with Fitzjohn. If Grieg's wife was out of the picture, what could he now expect from Grieg? More of what he had just experienced, no doubt. Unable to voice his thoughts to his sergeant, Fitzjohn sat back and said, 'How did you get on with your queries about Van Goren?'

'Silver Service cabs were very helpful, sir. Their records show that they picked the victim up three times last Friday. Once at 2pm from his home in Vaucluse, dropping him at St Vincent's Hospital in Darlinghurst, and then again just before 6pm, taking him to Raymond West's address on Phillip Street. From there, he took a third taxi to the Observatory, arriving around seven-thirty. I checked with the hospital. Van Goren had just finished a course of radiation treatment and received his prognosis. It wasn't good, sir. They'd given him a few months to live at the most.'

'Which gels with what Raymond West told us,' said Fitzjohn.

———>•<———

Fitzjohn arrived home that evening by taxi. At the gate, he stopped to extract letters from the box before starting along the garden path. As he did so, he could see a soft light emanating through the stained glass panel in the front door of his cottage. Finding the door ajar, he tentatively pushed it open. 'Sophie? Is that you?' As he spoke, his sister Meg appeared at the end of the hallway. Fitzjohn felt a sinking feeling. Ever since his late wife, Edith's, death eighteen months earlier, Meg had made it her quest in life to inflict her ministrations on him. Of course, it came as no surprise. He was well aware of Meg's propensity for over-involvement in other people's lives. This was demonstrated by her daughter Sophie's move to Sydney to escape her mother's unwanted attention.

'I didn't expect you, Meg,' he said, placing his briefcase and the mail on the hall table.

'That's because I decided to drop everything and fly up from Melbourne late this afternoon, Alistair.'

'Why would you do that? Is there something wrong?'

'Of course there's something wrong. Something is very wrong.'

With growing concern, Fitzjohn walked to where Meg stood in the kitchen doorway. 'What is it?'

'It's Sophie.'

A warning bell went off in Fitzjohn's head. 'As far as I know, Sophie's fine,' he replied.

'Well, that's where you're wrong, Alistair. She hasn't returned my calls or replied to any of my emails in days. Therefore, there is something the matter.'

'Meg, I think you're over-reacting. I spoke to Sophie last Thursday and she's fine. She's just busy moving house, that's all.'

'*Moving house?*' Fitzjohn took a step back as Meg's voice went up an octave. 'What do you mean, moving house?'

'Just what I said. She and a couple of her university friends have decided to share an apartment together.'

Meg wobbled on her high-heeled shoes and caught hold of the door-jamb. 'She can't do that,' she screamed. 'The only reason I agreed to her studying here in Sydney was that she'd live in university accommodation. Who are these, so-called, friends?'

'All I know is they're a couple of fellows in one of her tutorial groups.'

'A couple of *what*? You mean she's sharing accommodation with two males? *Alistair!* How could you let this happen? You're supposed to be looking after Sophie.'

Fitzjohn winced in despair at his over-bearing sister. 'Meg, Sophie is 22 years old, studying forensic medicine at Sydney University. She can look after herself, live where she likes, and with whomever she likes.'

'No she can't. What gave you that idea?' Meg turned back into the kitchen, the tea towel in her hand flying into the air. 'You do have a short memory, Alistair Fitzjohn. And you a policeman too. Have you forgotten that this time last year Sophie got arrested for being a public nuisance in that damned university sit-in? That alone demonstrates she can't look after herself.' Meg slumped down into a kitchen chair. 'This is worse than I thought. There's nothing else for it, she'll have to come home to Melbourne. I won't have my daughter cavorting around Sydney living who knows where.' Fitzjohn sighed and started toward the stairs. 'Where are you going?'

'Meg, it's late and I'm tired. I'm turning in. I have an early start in the morning.'

'But you can't. We have to talk about this because I need your support when I speak to Sophie in the morning.'

'I'm working on a case, Meg. I won't be taking any time off until it's solved.'

CHAPTER 5

With his camera equipment slung over one shoulder and a haversack over the other, photojournalist, Ben Carmichael, pushed his way through the crowded Cairo International Airport in an effort to secure a seat on a flight out as the city descended into chaos.

Torn between his desire to extend his assignment and remain to film the Arab Spring revolutionary wave of demonstrations, and his fiancée, Emma Phillips's wish that he return home, Ben moved unwillingly to the ticket counter. After all, Emma had left him with no false illusions when last they spoke by telephone a few days earlier. His constant absences were causing them to drift apart. Ben knew which he must choose because he was aware that once he found himself in the throes of an assignment, the adrenalin kicked in and everything other than what he caught on camera was forgotten.

It was late on Saturday evening when he climbed into a cab at Sydney's Kingsford Smith Airport on the last leg of his journey home. Weary, and yet tense, he stretched his long lean body out and tried to quell the images of the horrors he had witnessed during the past four weeks. At the same time, he contemplated the reception he was likely to receive from Emma.

When the taxi pulled up in front of the home they shared in Crows Nest, he paid the driver, slung his haversack over his shoulder, and walked through the garden to the front door. In the darkness he did not notice the junk mail spilling out of the letterbox at the gate nor see a yellow tinge to the grass on either side of the path. He just felt an overwhelming desire for his life to resume its normal path, at least for the next few weeks until his next photojournalism assignment. Hastening to the front door, he turned the key in the lock and walked inside. As he did so, a feeling of unease took hold. His haversack dropped from his shoulder, the thud as it hit the old oak floor filling the silence.

'Emma?' he called into the hot, stuffy atmosphere. 'Emma, darling, I'm home,' he called again up the stairwell. 'Hey, sleepy-head.' Ben took the stairs two at a time to the landing above where moonlight emanated through the front bedroom window, producing an eerie glow. A tingling sensation went through him. Tentatively, he walked into the room. The bed remained empty and undisturbed. 'Emma,' he whispered before his thoughts tumbled back to recall their last conversation. Had his relentless pursuit to capture, on camera, life as it happened, driven Emma away? He dived at the closet door, pulled it open and stood back. There, hung in meticulous order, were Emma's clothes. Relieved but puzzled, he made his way back down the stairs, stepped over his haversack and walked through to the kitchen. The steady drip of the tap into the sink of unwashed dishes caught his attention before his gaze went to his reflection in the glass patio doors. Sliding the doors open, he stepped outside. In the darkness, as if forgotten, clothes hung limp on the line. Emma's car space remained empty. Pulling his mobile phone from his pocket, he dialled her number.

"Your call could not be connected," answered the dispassionate recorded voice.

With growing desperation, he retraced his steps. As he reached the front hall, he heard a knock on the front door.

'Emma?' he yelled with a surge of relief.

'No, it's me,' a voice came from the darkened porch.

'Joanna? Is Emma with you?' he asked opening the screen door.

'No. I haven't heard from her since last week. I came over because I have to talk to you, Ben.'

'Is it about Emma?'

'No. Why do you keep asking about her?'

Ben noticed the uncharacteristic sharpness in Joanna's voice and hesitated. 'Because I'm worried. I just got home and she's not here.'

'Have you tried her mobile?'

'Yes. It's turned off.'

'Then I'd say she's at a movie.'

It was then that Ben took in the harried look on Joanna's face and the tears brimming her eyelids. 'What's wrong?' he asked, putting his hands on her shoulders and looking into her face. 'This isn't like you.' Ben fumbled in his pocket for a handkerchief. 'Here, wipe those tears and tell me about it.'

'It's Dad.'

Ben's eyes hardened. 'Joanna, please don't start on about that again. Especially tonight. The situation between Dad and me is never going to be resolved. I've accepted that. Why can't you?'

'It's not about your estrangement from Dad, Ben. I only wish it was.'

'Then what is it?'

'Dad suffered a heart attack early this morning. He's in the Intensive Care Unit at North Shore Hospital.' Ben gaped at his sister. 'The doctor's say it's touch and go whether he'll recover.' Joanna's voice broke and she began to weep.

Ben put his arm around her, a multitude of thoughts racing through his mind. 'I take it Laura is at the hospital.'

'Yes. She wanted you to know what's happened as soon as you arrived home.'

'How is she coping?' Ben thought of his step-mother, a stoic woman who doted on his father in every way.

'She's managing well under the circumstances. She knows Dad's chances aren't good, but as long as he's alive she has hope.' Joanna shook her head. 'She's such a positive person. I wish I was more like her. It helps at a time like this, and particularly with Dad being...'

'Being what? Joanna?'

Joanna glared at her brother. 'Being a suspect in a murder investigation.'

'A *what*?'

'Seems unbelievable, I know. It happened last night. Dad and Laura, together with the Hunts, hosted a cocktail party at the Observatory. It was for some of their company's clients. One of the guests was found dead in the grounds at the end of the evening. Someone, I don't know who it was, told the police that earlier in the evening they'd seen Dad arguing with the man who died.'

'Does Dad know this?'

'Yes. Laura and Dad left the venue early, before the body was found, but Emerson telephoned Dad later in the evening and told him.'

'When did Dad suffer his heart attack?'

Joanna hesitated before she said, 'Right after Emerson's call.'

'Was the man who died one of Dad's clients?'

'Laura doesn't think so. She thinks he must be one of Emerson's. His name was Peter Van Goren.' Joanna looked into Ben's face. 'Do you know him?'

'No. Should I?'

'Well, it's just that Mr Van Goren asked after you while I was talking to him last night. Are you sure you don't know him, Ben? He's not someone you'd forget in a hurry. He spoke with a slight foreign accent and walked with the aid of a cane. The cane alone might help you to recall the man if his name doesn't. It had the most exquisite silver handle in the shape of an eagle's head.'

Ben's shoulders slumped and his hand grabbed the banister.

'Are you all right?' asked Joanna in alarm. 'You've gone all white.'

Ben shook his head. 'It's jet lag. I haven't had much sleep. You'd better drive us to the hospital.'

'Okay. Are you going to leave Emma a note?'

'No. I'll keep trying her phone.'

———✦———

Laura Carmichael sat alone in the small waiting room, her hazel eyes sunken, her face pale. Even so, when she saw Ben standing in the doorway, a certain warmth transcended her sorrow. 'Ben, I'm so glad you're here at last,' she said, getting to her feet.

Ben caught Laura's trembling hands before putting his arms around the woman who had been a mother to him since he was a small boy. 'How's Dad?' he asked.

'Not good, I'm afraid. The doctors don't expect your father to survive.' Laura Carmichael's voice broke and she collapsed back into her chair. 'They've been forthright and I do appreciate that. They say his heart is far too damaged.' Silence ensued until Laura continued, 'You must both go in to see him while there's still time.'

Ben sat down in the chair next to Laura while Joanna hovered nearby. 'Do you think that's wise? You know how it is between Dad and me. The last thing I want is to upset him at a time like this.'

'You won't upset him, believe me,' replied Laura. 'Make your peace with him, Ben. Even if he's unable to respond, you need to resolve your troubles, for your own sake if not his.'

Ben glanced up at Joanna. 'You go first, Jo,' he said, before his thoughts drifted back to his last meeting with his father when the rift between them had been fuelled, yet again, by his refusal to invest in the property market. It all seemed so trivial in the face of what was now happening. He felt Laura's hand on his.

'Here's Joanna now. Go make your peace.'

———

Ben walked the short distance to the Intensive Care Unit. At the door, he hesitated, the years of recriminations between him and his father pouring through his mind. Tentatively, he opened the door and walked into the hushed atmosphere where those in attendance moved silently between patients in their constant vigil. His father's form lay still, his body monitored by machines, their steady beeps the only sound. Ben placed the palm of his hand over his father's. As he did so, Richard Carmichael's eyes fluttered. 'It's okay, Dad,' he said softly. 'You don't have to speak. I'll just sit here with you for a while.'

Richard Carmichael's lips moved. Ben bent over to listen to his whispered words. 'He told me you s... I'm sorry...' Tears glistened in Richard Carmichael's eyes as they closed.

Perplexed, Ben patted his father's hand. 'I'm sorry too, Dad.'

———

In the early hours of Sunday morning, Richard Carmichael slipped from this life, and as the sun appeared on the horizon, Laura, Ben and Joanna emerged from the hospital lost in their own thoughts.

'Are you sure you wouldn't like to come and stay with me for a few days, Laura,' asked Joanna as they reached her car. 'Thanks for the offer,' replied Laura, her face pale with sadness and fatigue. 'But I'd sooner be at home. I'll feel closer to Richard there with all his things around me.' She looked to Ben and caught his arm, concern on her face. 'Joanna told me about Emma. Have you been able to reach her yet?'

'No, but I'm sure it's because her phone's run out of battery.' As Ben said the reassuring words, a surge of anxiety went through him because he knew that Emma's fastidious nature would not allow that to happen. 'She'll be at home, I'm sure.'

In the growing humidity, Ben watched Joanna's car disappear into the traffic before he turned to make his way through the garden to the front door. In the light of day, he saw the junk mail spilling out of the letter box at the front gate, and the lawn tinged with yellow from lack of water before he lifted his gaze to the front door. It remained closed. His heart sank. If Emma were at home, that door would be open. Turning the key in the lock, he stepped inside. On the floor lay his haversack where he had dropped it the night before. 'Emma?' he called in hope. Amid the silence, he made his way into the living room, his eyes going to Emma's bright smile looking out at him from her photograph on the mantelpiece. 'Where are you?' he whispered. Clutching the frame, he slumped heavily into an armchair, his eyes glistening as his thoughts revisited their last conversation for a clue as to where she could be. When nothing came, he started to recall their first meeting in February 2011 during the Christchurch earthquake disaster. On assignment in New Zealand at the time, he had found himself attached to a group of journalists. Emma was one of them. Her resilience and spirit had drawn him to her at once and their romance blossomed amid the devastation and chaos. As he reflected, his mobile phone rang. 'Thank God,' he yelled, grabbing it from his pocket. 'Em? Is that you?'

'No, Ben, it's Audrey McIntyre, Emma's research assistant. I've been trying to contact Emma since last Saturday with no luck. That's why I thought I'd try you. Can you tell her that I've finished the research on one of the artists for her book? The other I should have done by the end of this coming week.'

'You say you've been trying to contact Emma since last Saturday?'

'Yes.'

'When did you last speak to her, Audrey?'

'Last Thursday night. We'd spent the better part of the day at the Mitchell Library doing research, so we had a bite to eat together in town after we'd finished. The last time I saw her was at Wynyard Station before she caught her train home. Why do you ask?'

'Because Emma wasn't here when I got home last night. I've been out of the country for the past month. I'm worried sick. Especially now since you say you haven't been able to reach her either.'

A moment of silence ensued on the line before Audrey said, 'No one has, Ben. I've asked everyone we know and no one has heard from Emma since last week.' Ben did not reply. 'Are you still there?' she asked.

'Yes. I'm here.'

'I think you should contact the police, don't you?'

'Yes. I'll do that.' As he spoke, the doorbell rang. 'I've got to go, Audrey. There's someone at the door. It might be news about Emma. I'll call you back.'

Ben lurched out into the front hall. Through the screen door stood a man of medium height wearing a dark grey suit and maroon tie. With him a tall ginger-haired younger man.

'Can I help you?' he asked, opening the door.

'Mr Ben Carmichael?'

'Yes. And you are?'

'Detective Chief Inspector Fitzjohn and this is Detective Sergeant Betts,' the man replied, his penetrating blue eyes looking through wire-framed glasses that sat on the bridge of his nose. 'We're from the New South Wales Police,' he continued emanating an air of authority despite his small stature.

A chill went through Ben as he peered at their warrant cards. 'Are you here about Emma Phillips, by any chance?'

'No. We'd like to speak to you in connection with a suspicious death at the Observatory last Friday evening.'

'Oh.' Taken aback, Ben pushed his haversack aside with his foot before standing back from the doorway. 'You'd better come in then.' He led the two police officers into the living room. 'Have a seat,' he said distractedly.

'We understand that since the incident at the Observatory, your father was taken to the hospital, Mr Carmichael,' said the Chief Inspector as he walked into the room. 'How is he?'

'He died early this morning.'

A look of concern came to the Chief Inspector's face. 'I'm very sorry to hear that. Please accept our condolences.'

Ben sat down in an armchair as the two officers settled themselves onto the sofa. The one with the ginger hair took out a notebook and pen from his inside coat pocket.

'It's regrettable that we have to disturb you at a time like this,' continued the Chief Inspector. 'But it's unavoidable, I'm afraid. Our investigation necessitates we carry on.'

Ben sat forward. 'Before we begin, can I ask you a question?'

'By all means.'

'Actually, I need some advice. It's nothing to do with your investigation but... it concerns my fiancée, Emma Phillips. You see I've been overseas for the past few weeks. I arrived back last night to find Emma gone. At the time, I thought she might be out with friends, but I've since learned that she hasn't been seen by any of them since last Thursday evening.' Ben hesitated. 'I'm worried.'

'When did you last speak to her, Mr Carmichael?' asked the Chief Inspector, sitting forward.

'One day last week. From Cairo.'

'And was everything all right between you at the time?'

Ben hesitated. 'Well, she did ask me to come home earlier than I'd planned and I told her that wasn't possible, but there was no reason to think she was going to leave me,' replied Ben, with indignation.

'Are any of her belongings missing from the house?'

'Not that I've noticed. Everything seems to be as it should be except her car is gone, and her handbag, of course.'

'Have you spoken to her family?'

'Not yet. There's just her father. He lives in New Zealand. He's recuperating from an operation at the moment, so I didn't want to worry him unnecessarily.'

'I take it then that Emma has a passport. Is it still here?'

'Oh. I didn't think to look.' Ben jumped up from his chair and lurched across the room to the small antique bureau in the corner. He pulled out the top drawer and sighed. 'It's still here.'

The Chief Inspector thought for a moment. 'Very well. In that case, I suggest we have Emma listed as a missing person.' Fitzjohn looked to his Sergeant. 'Betts, can you get the wheels in motion while I speak to Mr Carmichael about the other matter?'

'Yes, sir.'

As the sergeant left the room, the Chief Inspector turned back to Ben. 'The Missing Persons Unit will make routine checks of your fiancée's bank accounts and credit cards to see if any withdrawals have been made since Thursday night. They'll also check her telephone's activity since that time.'

'I feel so helpless.' Ben sat down again and wiped his face with his hands.

'We'll do all we can to find her, Mr Carmichael.'

'Thank you. I appreciate it.' Ben paused before he continued. 'I take it you're here to talk to me about my father. My sister, Joanna, told me that he's a suspect in your investigation. Can I ask why?'

'Your father is a person of interest, Mr Carmichael, as is everyone who attended the cocktail party at the Observatory, but your father is of particular interest to us because he was seen arguing with the deceased during the course of the evening.'

Ben grimaced. 'Who told you that?'

'I'm afraid I'm not at liberty to say.'

'So what is it you want to ask me? Obviously you know I wasn't there.'

'Yes. We're aware of that. Even so, I'd like to know whether you knew the victim, Peter Van Goren. Apparently, he was a foreign gentleman. Spoke with a European accent. He also used a walking cane.' Once again, Ben trembled at the mention of the cane. 'The reason I ask is because when he arrived at the function, he asked after you.'

'Mmm. So my sister said, but I can assure you, I didn't know the man.'

'I see. Well, in that case, I must ask you to accompany DS Betts and myself to the morgue in Parramatta, to make a visual identification of the body.'

'Is that altogether necessary?'

'Under the circumstances, I'm afraid it is,' replied the Chief Inspector.

CHAPTER 6

'From the look on Ben Carmichael's face when I pulled back the sheet covering Peter Van Goren's body, I'd say he knew the victim.' Betts pushed himself from the filing cabinet and sat down in front of Fitzjohn's desk.

Fitzjohn took his glasses off and placed them down in front of him before he rocked back in his chair. 'Mmm. There was definitely a reaction there, but it might simply have been the sight of the corpse. After all, it's not an easy sight for you and me, Betts, let alone the uninitiated.'

'But is he uninitiated, sir? I've read up on Ben Carmichael and seen some of his work. He's one of the best known photojournalists in the world. He's covered the Iraq war, Afghanistan, in fact, the worst trouble spots there are. You'd think he'd have seen a lot of violence and death.'

'No doubt he has,' replied Fitzjohn. 'But does one ever get to the point where being confronted with death isn't a shock to the system?' Fitzjohn looked at his young sergeant before he continued. 'Okay. Let's take Ben Carmichael's apparent shock at seeing the corpse as a sign that he did know the victim. It would explain the reason he's our victim's beneficiary and why Van Goren asked after him at the cocktail party last Friday evening. But...' Fitzjohn held up his right index finger. 'On the other hand, if Ben Carmichael is telling the truth, and he didn't know Peter Van Goren, then there has to be a connection of some kind that hasn't surfaced yet. In other words, a reason why Van Goren left Ben Carmichael his entire estate.'

'We just have to find out what it is,' added Betts.

'Yes, and that's why we need as much information as possible on Van Goren.'

'I've got Williams working on that, sir.'

'Williams?' Fitzjohn shot a look at Betts. 'I thought he'd been moved permanently to Kings Cross Local Area Command.'

'He had, but Chief Superintendent Grieg requested he be transferred back here to Day Street, sir.'

'How does Williams feel about that?'

'He seems okay with it,' replied Betts with a shrug.

Fitzjohn's thoughts went back to his own secondment to Kings Cross Police Station the previous autumn where he had met up with Detective Senior Constable Williams. At the time, Williams's transfer appeared to have transformed him from a man of sullen disposition, into an ebullient character. Not only had he received a promotion to Senior Constable, he told Fitzjohn, but he had also been released from Day Street Station and the oppressive Chief Superintendent Grieg. Was it all a sham? Had Williams been the mole that

Fitzjohn suspected Grieg had planted at Kings Cross at that time? If so, his problems with Grieg could only get worse with Williams now back at Day Street.

Pushing the thought aside, Fitzjohn rose from his chair and started to pace the floor. 'Let's go through everything we have so far, Betts. We need to plan where we go from here.'

Betts took his notebook from his inside coat pocket and studied it. 'Well, firstly, the hosts of last Friday night's cocktail party, the Carmichael's and the Hunt's, as well as all the guests, deny knowing the victim, Peter Van Goren. Probably not surprising since Van Goren didn't appear on the guest list. Secondly, it was recorded that a number of the guests witnessed Richard Carmichael arguing with the victim during the course of the evening.'

'And then there's the fact that those we have spoken to who did know the victim, such as Van Goren's housekeeper, Ida Clegg, and his solicitor, Raymond West, have only known Van Goren since the early 1980s,' put in Fitzjohn. 'Why is that, do you think?'

'Perhaps previous to that Peter Van Goren lived overseas,' offered Betts. 'After all, to me, the name Van Goren sounds Dutch. Maybe he migrated to Australia in the 1980s.'

'Mmm. It's certainly a possibility.' Fitzjohn stopped pacing. 'What else do we have?'

'That's it, sir. We're back to why Peter Van Goren left his entire estate to Ben Carmichael.'

'So, our questions are what, Betts?'

Betts sat back. 'One, who at that cocktail party is lying about not knowing Peter Van Goren? Two, what was Richard

Carmichael's argument with Van Goren about? And, three, what connection did the victim have with Ben Carmichael?'

'And why does Van Goren only appear in people's lives from the early 1980s,' added Fitzjohn, sitting down again. 'What did you find out about our tennis player, Theodora Hunt?'

Betts turned to the next page of his notebook. 'She has her own business, sir.'

'She does?'

'Yes. A shop in Willoughby called. *Fabrique en France*, meaning "Made in France". *Ou vous trouver inspiration francaise articles ménages adaptes a chaque maison*, meaning, "Where you can find French inspired homewares to suit every home."'

'I'm impressed, Betts. I didn't realise that you're bilingual.'

'School boy French, sir. You never know when it can be useful.' Betts gave a quick smile and looked back at his notebook. 'By all accounts, the business is very successful. It has a yearly turn-over of just over one million dollars.' Betts paused. 'I'm surprised to be honest. That she's in business, I mean, because to me she didn't come across as the brightest candle in the shop.'

'You mean you wouldn't have thought she'd have the acumen to run a business, let alone a highly successful one?' asked Fitzjohn.

'I suppose that's a more polite way of putting it. Of course, it could be what she wants us to think.'

'It can't be discounted,' replied Fitzjohn. 'Guilt can produce all sorts of odd behaviour. We'll speak to her again,

Betts. This time without her husband present. We might learn something.'

As Betts left the office, the Duty Sergeant appeared. 'There's someone to see you, Chief Inspector. Your niece, I believe.'

'Sophie? Show her in, Sergeant.' Fitzjohn got to his feet as Sophie walked into the room, her usual cheery smile absent.

'Hello, Uncle Alistair.'

'Sophie dear, I'm glad you're here. You've come about your mother, haven't you?'

'Yes. She rang first thing this morning when I was on my way to my first lecture.' Sophie slumped down into a chair. 'She's demanding that I return to Melbourne with her.'

'I know. She told me last night when I arrived home. I'm sorry, Sophie. I probably should have let you know but to tell you the truth, I didn't want to interfere. I think the time has come for you to stand up to your mother.'

'That's easier said than done.'

'I know it is, but it's the only way, I'm afraid. Unless you want this kind of thing to continue.'

Sophie sighed. 'You're right. I know you are. It's just that when Mum goes on about what I should be doing... well... my confidence just flies out the window.' Sophie shrugged. 'But, I'll give it a try this evening. I have lectures all after-noon.' She looked at the plastic bag on her lap. 'Oh, there's one more thing. Is Martin around?'

'No. He's out doing detective work for me. Why?'

'Because I wanted to thank him and return this. It's his sweater.'

Fitzjohn's browed wrinkled. 'What are you doing with my sergeant's sweater?'

'He left it behind the other night when he was helping us move.'

'He did, did he?'

CHAPTER 7

The door creaked and a bell sounded as Fitzjohn and Betts walked into the old Federation style building that housed *Fabrique en France*. With its high patterned ceilings and leadlight windows, the walls covered in tapestries and old photographic prints of Paris, its interior exuded an atmosphere of times past. The two officers walked amongst the soft furnishing and tables filled with bric-a-brac to where Theodora Hunt could be seen at the far end of the shop, talking to a customer. Wearing a tight floral dress over her buxom frame, her blonde locks tied up in a matching scarf, she excused herself and bustled over to where they waited.

'Good morning, Chief Inspector.'

'Morning, Mrs Hunt,' replied Fitzjohn. 'We'd like to speak to you again if we may.'

'Of course, although I doubt I can add anything to what Emerson and I have already told you.'

'Be that as it may, Mrs Hunt, we wondered whether you might have recalled something else relating to Richard

Carmichael's argument with Peter Van Goren. For instance, did you get a sense that they knew each other?'

Theodora's eyes darted from Fitzjohn to Betts before she glanced over to her customer who now stood at the counter. 'Will you excuse me for just one minute while I serve that woman?'

'She knows something,' said Fitzjohn under his breath as Theodora scurried away. 'But I have a feeling we're not going to find out what it is. Not today, anyway.' Amid Theodora's continuous prattle to her customer, Fitzjohn and Betts browsed the knick knacks on the many shelves before she rejoined them.

'I'm sorry about that,' she said. 'It tends to get busy at this time of day. Now, where were we?'

'You were about to tell us what you gleaned from Richard Carmichael's argument with Peter Van Goren,' replied Fitzjohn.

'Oh, yes. Well, I can't say I gleaned anything other than what I told you previously. I heard Ben's name mentioned and Richard telling Mr Van Goren to leave the premises. I'm afraid that's all.'

'Did Richard Carmichael argue with anyone else that evening?'

'Well, since you mention it, he did have words with his half-brother, Sebastian, before he left the marquee to speak to the caterer about the food presentation.'

'You mean they quarrelled?' asked Fitzjohn.

'Yes.'

'Do you know what that was about?'

'No, because Richard was trying to keep his voice down. But I don't think I've ever seen him look quite so angry. He's usually such a placid person. Or at least he was.'

'Did the two brothers' normally disagree?'

'I've never known them to argue, but you never really know what goes on behind closed doors, do you, Chief Inspector? If anything, Sebastian has always seemed to have been a great support for Richard. Especially when Richard's first wife, Rachael, died.'

'Oh? When did she pass away?' asked Fitzjohn with growing interest.

Theodora thought for a moment. 'It must be close to thirty years ago if not more. 1983, I think. Or was it '84. At any rate, it was when their children, Ben and Joanna were quite young. A dreadful tragedy. Made worse by the way in which she died.'

'Why? What happened to her, Mrs Hunt?'

'She fell from the top of a cliff that ran along the edge of the family's property at Whale Beach. What made things worse is that her body wasn't found until a couple of days later, further up the coast.' Theodora became animated. 'At the time, there was talk that the gardener did it.'

'The gardener?'

'Yes. Ridiculous, of course. Henry wouldn't have hurt a fly.'

'Then why do you think he was thought to be guilty?' asked Fitzjohn.

'Because he disappeared on the day Rachael died.'

Fitzjohn and Betts left *Fabrique en France* and made their way along the footpath to their car. 'You were right, sir. I think Mrs Hunt was more open without her husband present.'

'Mmm. I doubt we would have learnt about Richard Carmichael's first wife or about his argument with his half-brother if Emerson Hunt had been there. And even though Rachael Carmichael's death isn't relevant to our investigation, I want to take a look at the Coroner's Report. It might help to give us a bit of background on the Carmichael family.'

'Yes, sir.'

'Also, I want to speak to Sebastian Newberry again because I'd really like to know what he and his brother argued about on Friday night. I seem to remember him telling us he has an interior design business.'

'That's right,' replied Betts, climbing into the car. 'Ultra Design. It's in Crows Nest. On Chandos Street.'

Fitzjohn and Betts walked into the Ultra Design showroom to find Sebastian Newberry with a young couple near a display of curtain materials. He looked around when he heard the door open. Impeccably dressed in a dark blue pin striped suit and bright red tie, he excused himself and walked toward them.

'Good morning, gentlemen.'

'Good morning, Mr Newberry,' replied Fitzjohn. 'We'd like to speak to you again if we may.'

'Not the best timing,' said Newberry, looking around. 'As you can see, we're quite busy at the moment.'

'We're quite busy too, Mr Newberry, endeavouring to solve a murder.'

Newberry glared at Fitzjohn before he called to his young assistant at the reception desk. 'Jacinta, my dear, can you take over, please?'

'Yes, Mr Newberry.'

Newberry turned back to Fitzjohn and Betts. 'We can talk in my office. This way.' They left the showroom and entered a spacious room, its modern furniture, neutral tones and marble floor exuding the same stark minimalism as the showroom. He gestured toward two chrome-framed white plastic chairs in front of his desk before sitting down himself.

'You appear to have a thriving business, Mr Newberry,' said Fitzjohn.

'We do, Chief Inspector, probably because we're a multi-faceted operation. Not only do we deal with interior design and decorating, but architectural services as well.' Newberry gave a quick smile and sat back in his chair. 'Although, having said that, a great deal of our success is due to my brother, Richard. He referred many of his clients to us.' Newberry paused. 'I take it you've heard of Richard's passing.'

'We have. It's most regrettable,' replied Fitzjohn.

'It is, and in light of that fact, I hope he can now be removed from your list of suspects. My brother was a decent man, Chief Inspector. Richard would never have perpetrated such a crime on another human being, I can assure you.'

'We understand your concern, Mr Newberry. However, I'm afraid everyone who attended the cocktail party last Friday evening will remain "persons of interest" until our investigation is complete.'

'Well, I hope that's soon because I don't want my brother's memory sullied by what happened that night. Especially since he's no longer here to defend himself.'

'I take it you and your brother were close.'

'We were. Largely because we were both left fatherless at a young age. My father, Edmund Newberry, died in a car accident when I was just two. My mother was still quite young at the time and remarried my father's best friend as it happened. Desmond Carmichael. But it didn't last. Desmond left us shortly after Richard was born.'

'We're led to believe that your brother spoke to you straight after his argument with Peter Van Goren. Did he tell you what their argument was about,' asked Fitzjohn.

Newberry shifted in his chair. 'No. I didn't even know they'd argued until Theodora Hunt mentioned it to you on Friday night.'

'I see. Well, in that case, can you tell me what you and your brother spoke about?'

'It was business, that's all. Richard said he had a client who was interested in having a property renovated.'

'So you yourselves didn't argue.'

'Certainly not. Why? Has someone told you we did?'

Fitzjohn ignored Newberry's question. 'It helps if those we interview tell us the truth, Mr Newberry. We'll leave it there for now.'

CHAPTER 8

Ablackbird's call resonated in the morning's half light, and Ben stirred, the escape he had found in sleep, ending. As he dozed, thoughts drifted through his mind. His father's anxiety as he lay dying, Peter Van Goren's ashen face when the sheet fell away, and Emma. What of Emma? The thump of the morning paper hitting the front door sounded and Ben made his way downstairs. Opening the door, he found Joanna about to knock. She smiled through the wisps of fair hair falling from her pony tail and handed him the paper.

'I didn't hear from you last night so I take it all's well and Emma was here when you got home.' When Ben did not reply, Joanna gaped. 'She was just out at a movie, wasn't she?'

'No. I've not heard from her, and neither have any of her friends. Not since last Thursday.' Ben rubbed the back of his neck. 'The police have her listed as missing.'

'Oh, Ben. I'm so sorry. You must be worried sick.' Joanna looked at her brother's dishevelled appearance and his haversack still on the floor next to the stairs. 'I wish you'd called. I'd have come straight over.'

'You needed to be with Laura, and besides, events took over and I had to go out. The police wanted me to view Peter Van Goren's body to see if I could identify him.'

Joanna grimaced. 'And were you able to?'

'No.' Ben's thoughts returned to the morgue and the sense of dread and sorrow that seared through him when he had seen Van Goren's face. All at once he hit the rolled up newspaper against the side of his leg. 'Would you like coffee?'

Joanna nodded and followed her brother through to the kitchen where he tossed the paper onto the large wooden table in the centre of the room. 'I hope you don't mind instant. I've never been home long enough to come to grips with the workings of that "state of the art" espresso machine over there. Emma's the coffee maker.' He poured boiling water into two mugs and brought them to the table before slumping down into a chair. 'God only knows what's happened to her.'

'Have you spoken to her dad in New Zealand?'

'Not yet. With his recent health problems, I didn't want to alarm him unnecessarily but now, with no news of Emma... I'll call him this morning.' Ben sighed. 'I've got to try and find her, Joanna. I can't just sit here and do nothing.'

Joanna patted her brother's hand. 'I know it's difficult, but I don't know what else you can do but wait until you hear from the police.' A moment of silence followed as they both sipped their coffee. 'Have you spoken to your neighbours? After all, one of them might have seen Emma leave in her car.'

'I did a door-knock. The neighbours I spoke to haven't noticed Emma since last week sometime. The only one I wasn't able to speak to is Ron next door because he's away. I'll talk to him when he gets back.' Ben looked at his sister. 'I'm not very good company, I know. My mind's in a bit of a fog.' Ben took another sip of his coffee. 'How's Laura?'

'She's coping - quietly. The fact that she's Dad's executrix is a distraction because there is a lot she has to do, as well as the funeral arrangements. I have a feeling it'll be after the funeral that the fact that Dad is gone will hit her.' Joanna stared at her mug of coffee, turning it around as she did so. 'It doesn't seem real to me either. Not yet.' Joanna looked up. 'Anyway, I'm staying with her for the time being. I thought a bit of company wouldn't go astray. For either of us.' Joanna prodded the pile of letters that sat with the newspaper in the middle of the table. 'Aren't you going to open your mail?'

'No. I'll open it later.'

Joanna studied her brother's face. 'Ben, you have to keep going. You can't let things slip,' she said as she spread the letters out with her index finger. 'This one's from a solicitor's office. West Longmire & Associates. It could be important.'

Ben picked up the monogrammed envelope. 'Why would a solicitor be writing to me?'

'Why don't you open it and find out?'

Grudgingly, Ben ran his finger along the inside top of the envelope and took out the folded sheet of soft vellum writing paper. His eyes scanned the letter. 'What the heck!'

'Is it bad news or good?'

'I'm not sure. Listen to this.'

Dear Mr Carmichael

I wish to advise that you are named as a beneficiary in the last will and testament of my client, Peter Van Goren.

Please contact my office at your earliest convenience to arrange an appointment so that we can discuss this matter.

Yours sincerely
Raymond West
Senior Partner
West Longmire & Associates
Barristers & Solicitors

Ben handed the letter to Joanna.

'Are you sure you didn't recognise Peter Van Goren when you saw him at the morgue?' she asked, taking the letter in her hand.

'Of course I'm sure. I've never seen the man in my life before.' Ben shook as the image of Van Goren's wax-like face flashed through his mind.

'Well, it seems he knew you,' she replied as she read the letter for herself. 'You don't make complete strangers beneficiaries in your will. And he did ask me about you at the cocktail party on Friday night, remember?'

As Joanna spoke, the doorbell rang. 'That might be the police with news.' Ben jumped up from his chair. Moments later he returned followed by a dark haired young woman in her late thirties.

'Joanna, this is Audrey McIntyre, Emma's research assistant. Audrey, my sister.'

Audrey extended her hand to Joanna. 'Pleased to meet you, Joanna. I was hoping you'd heard from Emma, but Ben says not.' Audrey adjusted her dark-rimmed glasses and sat down at the kitchen table before placing her handbag on her lap. 'I wish I could be of more help,' she continued. 'But as I told Ben yesterday, the last time I spoke to Emma was Thursday night.' Audrey adjusted her glasses again. 'I'm also sorry to hear about your Dad. I saw it on the news last night.' She looked to Ben. 'I had no idea what had happened to him when we spoke on the phone. I'm so sorry.'

'You weren't to know,' said Ben joining them at the table. 'I take it the police contacted you about Emma?'

'Yes. They came to see me yesterday afternoon. I tried to remember as much as I could about the last time I saw her. I told you Emma and I spent Thursday afternoon at the Mitchell Library, didn't I?'

'Yes, you did. You're helping her with research for her book on Australian artists, aren't you?' said Ben.

'That's right. I've been researching two South Australian painters for her. Did you know that Emma had decided to also include your mother's work in the book?'

'She did mention it,' replied Ben. 'But I told her I didn't think it was a good idea.'

'Oh.' Audrey's brow wrinkled. 'Then I guess I've let the cat out of the bag.'

'Why do you say that?' asked Ben.

'Because as far as I know, Emma's going ahead with it. She's already done quite a lot of research into your mother's work and her life as an artist. The only thing she hasn't been able to do yet is to visit her studio at Lane's End. She wanted to go there and take photographs, but for that she told me she needed your father's permission.'

'That's right, and I doubt he'd have given it. None of the family has been back to Lane's End since our mother died.' Ben glanced at Joanna. 'The property's been closed up since that time. Thirty years.'

'Mmm. That's what Emma said, and that's why she approached your step-mother Laura, rather than your Dad.' A look of surprise crossed Ben's face as he recalled telling Emma that her request to visit Lane's End would, undoubtedly, be refused by his father and that to pursue the matter would only cause her more disappointment. At the time, he had sensed her dismay in his lack of support, but how could he explain his father's sensitivities about Lane's End. After all, what had happened there, years ago, was only a memory that lurked in the darkest recesses of his mind and had done so for as long as he could remember. A shiver went through him as it always did when his thoughts drifted into the past with its shadows and untold truths. 'She was a bit miffed actually that Laura hadn't got back to her,' continued Audrey.

'That's probably because she was waiting for the right moment to bring the subject up with Dad. It's always been a closed topic with him,' replied Ben.

'Oh, I didn't know that. It would have made it difficult for your step-mother to broach the subject then.'

'Did Emma say how else she planned to conduct her research about our mother, Audrey?' asked Joanna.

'No, although she did say that she'd spoken to a woman who'd known your Mum. I think her name was Theodora.'

'Theodora Hunt?' chimed Ben and Joanna.

'Yes. That's it. You know her then?'

'She's the wife of our father's business partner, Emerson Hunt.'

Ben shut the front door behind Audrey McIntyre and returned to the kitchen. 'So, Emma went ahead with including our mother in her book after I told her it wasn't a good idea,' said Ben, sitting down at the kitchen table again. 'I guess I shouldn't be surprised, but I'd hoped she'd listened for a change.'

'Saying it's not a good idea isn't telling her not to, Ben,' replied Joanna.

'Well, that's what I meant.'

'Then you should have spelt it out. Emma is very strong willed. Anyway, why didn't you want our mother included in the book? I think it's a wonderful idea. By all accounts she was a talented artist.'

'I don't doubt she was. I just thought it would cause more friction between Dad and me.'

Joanna reflected for a moment. 'Mmm. You're probably right. Let's face it, Dad never did get over you choosing a photographic career instead of academia, did he? But I did think that when you became so successful at what you do, he'd have eased off a bit.' Joanna paused. 'I wonder what was really at the bottom of his contempt.'

'What do you mean?'

'I mean that I believe there was another reason that Dad made life difficult for you. If you think about it, things weren't much better between the two of you even before you went to university.'

Joanna was right, of course. Things had never been good between him and Dad. Why was that? Did it have something to do with the past? After all, he knew that Lane's End, once the Carmichael's summer house by the sea, was a source of sorrow for his father. It was almost as if he wanted to erase it from his memory. Ben thought of his father's last words. "He told me you s... I'm sorry...". What had his words meant? Was he saying sorry for the hostility that had existed between them or did they have some other special significance? 'Well, whatever it was, Joanna, it doesn't matter now, does it?'

'No, I guess not.' Joanna picked up the solicitor's letter again. 'What are you going to do about this letter?'

Ben shook his head. 'I can't deal with that right now.'

'I think you must. After all, Dad is still a suspect in this man's murder. You might be able to find out why he asked after you.'

Ben shook his head. 'It'll have to wait, Jo. I've got to find Emma first.'

CHAPTER 9

With his dark wavy hair falling over his forehead, his skin browned by the Middle Eastern sun, Ben Carmichael cut a striking figure as he walked into *Fabrique en France* later that morning. He found Theodora humming to herself while rearranging a table full of bric-a-brac, lost in her own world. A friendly woman in a light kind of way, Ben had always seen her as possessing an innocent gaiety. She had never professed to have been close to his mother, but he was comforted in the knowledge that she was, nevertheless, a link.

Theodora looked around when the bell on the door rang, her face full of concern. 'Ben, I'm so glad you've come by. I did plan to call you today. I heard about Emma on the news. I'm so sorry, darling. Is there any word?'

'No, Theo. Nothing yet. I'm just trying to retrace Emma's steps before she disappeared. One of her friends said she came to see you recently.' Ben sat down on a stool next to the table of bric-a-brac.

'That's right, she did. It was last Monday morning around ten o'clock. We'd never met before. She's a lovely girl, Ben. I liked her immediately. Very straight forward and to the point. A good attribute to have when you're a freelance journalist, I imagine.'

'What did you want to see you about, Theo?'

'She wanted to ask me about your mother because she said she plans to include her in a book she's working on about Australian artists. She said she hoped I could provide her with some background information on her early work. I was able to help her with background, of course, but as far as her work was concerned, I failed miserably. I can't say I've ever been interested in any form of art so I took little interest in your mother's talent. All I could tell Emma was that your mother spent a lot of time at Lane's End and that she used the cottage for her studio. And that she adored the place, of course. Anyway, that wasn't quite what Emma had in mind, so I suggested she speak to your Uncle Sebastian. After all, he'd known your mum the longest.'

'I didn't know that,' replied Ben, with growing interest. 'But then I know very little about my mother. Other than Laura giving Joanna and me the barest of facts, no one's ever spoken of her.'

'So I understand. It's almost as though your Dad wanted to erase all memory of her, so painful was her death to him. I must say, it did become clear, early on, to Emerson and me that there wasn't to be any discussion about her and the way in which she died. *Ever*. So, of course, we honoured your father's wishes.'

'What do you know about her death, Theo?'

'The little I do know, Amanda Marsh told me. She was your mother's housekeeper at the time. But you know that.

She said she and your mother had taken you and Joanna to Lane's End for the long weekend. It was a Friday morning so your Dad was to follow later in the day after he'd finished work in the city. I don't know all the details, only that your mother was found to be missing that afternoon by Sebastian. At the time, the police suspected foul play because your parents' gardener went missing after the alarm was raised.'

'Gardener? I don't remember any gardener.'

'That's not surprising. You couldn't have been much more than six years old at the time.'

'What happened when the police found him?' asked Ben.

'Well, that's just it. They didn't.' Theodora looked back down at the table she was rearranging.

'So, what happened with the police investigation?'

'As far as I know, the case was never solved.'

'Meaning no real closure for my father.'

'No,' replied Theodora, thoughtfully. 'I think that was one of the most difficult things for him. Not knowing what really happened to your mother. Whether she fell or...'

Ben sensed Theodora's discomfort. 'You mean it was never made clear how she died?'

Theodora looked awkwardly at Ben. 'I'm really not the one you should talk to about this. Really, I'm not. Whatever I know, or think I know, I've heard from others.

'Tell me anyway.'

Theodora sighed. 'All I know is that the Coroner couldn't decide whether your mother had accidentally fallen from the cliff, was pushed or...'

'Or what?' Ben glared at Theodora. 'You mean it was thought she might have committed suicide? *God!* No wonder

Dad never got over it. He'd have wondered whether he'd done something to cause her death.'

'I believe he did,' replied Theodora. 'A terrible thought for him to live with.'

Ben got to his feet. 'Thanks for telling me, Theo. It helps make some sense of a lot of the past.'

'It hasn't helped as far as Emma is concerned though, has it? Perhaps if you have a word with Sebastian. I'm sure Emma planned to speak to him after she left here because as I said, he'd known your mother the longest. Ever since art school when they were quite young. And of course, that's how your parents eventually met. Through Sebastian.'

Ben left Theodora to rearrange her tables, what she had told him about his mother and the circumstances of her death, rushing through his head. In a way, it helped to explain his father's resolve never to speak of that time, but it did not explain the animosity that had existed between them. Perhaps it had nothing to do with the past after all. He also pondered Sebastian's part in all this. By all accounts, not only his father's half-brother but his mother's friend since they were young, and the person who found her missing the day she died. It surprised him, therefore, that Sebastian had never played a part in his and Joanna's life, remaining all but a stranger. Nevertheless, he hoped that if Emma had spoken to Sebastian, it might bring to light a clue as to her whereabouts.

———❦———

The morning sun filtered through the windows of the Ultra Design showroom giving a little warmth to the otherwise austere modernistic surroundings. Ben could only remember being in the showroom once before, as a teenager when he had accompanied his father. It was perhaps one of the few times he had come into contact with Sebastian.

'Can I help you?'

Ben looked past the displays of interior furnishings to the far end of the room to see a slim young woman with shoulder length auburn hair, sitting at a desk. 'I'm here to see Mr Newberry.'

'Is he expecting you, Mr...?'

'Carmichael. Ben Carmichael, and no, he isn't.'

'Very well. I'll have a word with Mr Newberry. If you'd care to take a seat, I won't be long.' She gave a quick smile and gestured to the chair in front of her desk.

A few minutes later Sebastian emerged from an inner office. Dressed in a light grey suite and blue and white striped tie, Ben realised he would not have recognised him if they had passed on the street. There was also a sense of grimness about him. Obviously, his father's death had affected Sebastian greatly.

'Ben,' he said, extending his hand. 'It's been a long time. Come through to my office. We can talk there.'

Sebastian's office lay at the back of the building where the warmth of the morning sun could not reach. It remained, therefore, subject to the stark minimalist style that he obviously preferred. He gestured to one of the chairs in front of his desk before he sat down himself. 'I take it you're here about your father's funeral arrangements. Of course I will help in any way I can.'

'That's very kind,' replied Ben, settling himself into a chair. 'But it's not that I'm here about. You probably haven't heard that my fiancée, Emma Phillips, has gone missing.'

Sebastian's face darkened. '*What!* But it's only a few days ago that she was here.'

'So she did come to see you. Theodora said she might have.'

'Yes. It was last Monday. She said she's working on a book about artists and wanted to include your mother. I told her I thought it a marvellous idea. Your mother was so talented. Her work shouldn't be forgotten.'

Ben sensed an enthusiasm in Sebastian's demeanour as he spoke about his mother. 'I wish I could remember her. You obviously knew her well.'

'I did, and that's why I encouraged Emma. She mentioned that she wanted to go to Lane's End to see Ivy Cottage.'

'I can't imagine that my father would have agreed to that, do you?' asked Ben.

'Not really. No. But I didn't say that to Emma. She seemed so keen. I hoped she might be able to persuade him.'

'Did she happen to mention what her other plans were? If she did, it might give me some clue as to what's happened to her.'

'I'm sorry, Ben. She only spoke of her wish to go to Lane's End. She seemed bent on the idea.'

Ben, his face displaying his growing anguish, sat at a coffee shop's outside table in Crows Nest and mulled over his conversation with Sebastian. With no new lead to follow, he felt powerless to help Emma when she might need him the most. He looked up when the waiter approached to take his order and saw Joanna and Laura walking along the sidewalk towards him.

'Just coffee, please,' he told the waiter before getting to his feet.

'Ben. We've just been around to your house to see you,' said Joanna as they all sat down. 'Is there any news about Emma?'

'Not from the police, but I did manage to catch up with my neighbour, Ron Evans. He said he saw Emma leave the house in her car early on Saturday morning. It seems he might be the last person to have seen her.' Ben drummed his fingers on the arm of his chair. 'The rest of the morning I've spent speaking to Theodora and Sebastian.'

Ben recounted his meetings.

'So Emma spoke to Theodora and Sebastian too about going to Lane's End,' said Laura, an edge to her voice. 'She came to see me as well.' Laura sighed. 'I'm sorry, Ben, I should have told you about it, but with all that's happened, I didn't think. My mind's been in such a state of confusion lately. Emma came to see me because she wanted permission to go and look at Ivy Cottage. I never found the right moment to broach the subject with your father although I doubt he would have agreed. I don't even think he'd have wanted Emma to include your mother in the book. Her memory was so painful for him.'

'I think you're right,' replied Ben. 'Did she say anything else that might give me a clue as to what could have happened to her?'

'No. I can't think of anything. She just asked me about visiting the cottage and I said I'd get back to her. That's all.'

'I wonder if she got sick of waiting and went there anyway? She's never been blessed with a great deal of patience when she really wants something,' said Ben.

'She wouldn't do that,' said Joanna. 'Would she?'

'No. She wouldn't have gone without permission. She knew how your Dad felt about the place.' Laura patted Ben's hand.

'Mmm. You're probably right, but... I think I'll take a drive out there anyway. Just to settle my mind.'

Ben turned off the main road onto a narrow lane, and with dust billowing up behind his car, he continued on at a slow pace looking for the entrance to Lane's End. He caught sight of its tall, rusted, wrought iron gates, sagging on their remaining hinges, partially hidden amongst overgrown bushes. He brought the car to a standstill and peered beyond the stone wall bordering the property to a weed-ridden driveway that curved before it disappeared through a row of tall cedars. Gingerly, he drove in, the car tyres crunching on the last remaining pieces of gravel. When the majestic edifice of the house his parents had once called their "home by the sea", came into view, his heart quickened. Built in an era of grand design, it dominated the landscape. The river stone walls once a feature of beauty, were now hidden behind ivy, the tentacles finding their way into every crevice and intertwining with the last remnants of a mandevilla vine that clung to life across the wide verandah.

Transfixed by memories of childish laughter and long hot summer days, he climbed out of the car, his gaze taking in the vast grounds and what, as a small boy, had seemed a limitless paradise of adventure. These reflections left him, however, when he made his way onto the verandah to peer in through one of the bay windows. There, frozen in time, he could see the living room as it had been thirty years earlier, a reminder of life once lived inside its walls. Pulling back, and with a certain amount of inquisitiveness, he grappled with the screen door and levered it open, dust flying in his face as he did so. Fumbling with the bunch of keys that Laura had given to him earlier in the day, he tried several before the front door, now warped and grey beneath peeling paint, swung open. Hesitantly he stepped into the hot dry atmosphere and made his way along the hallway, each floorboard squeaking under his tread. It was then that a sense of apprehension, mixed with panic, took hold. A chill went through his body, despite the heat, while visions of the past danced before him.

'What's happening to me?' he heard himself shout.

Struggling back outside, he slammed the door behind him. On the verandah and with his heart pounding, he stood for a few minutes until his panic dissipated. Taking a deep breath, he descended the steps, and with childhood recollections to guide him, made his way along the side of the house on a path that he sensed would lead deeper into Lane's End, and eventually to Ivy Cottage.

Gingerly he picked his way through the overgrown weeds and bushes until, at the rear of the house, a small stone building on the edge of the tree-line came into view. Ben started to recall the landscape and with it, long forgotten memories filtered through his mind.

'The gardener's cottage. I remember him now,' he muttered. Ben stood staring at the small building as if waiting to learn more. Presently, he walked on into the trees along what had once been a well-worn path. Beads of sweat sprung from his brow in the hot humid atmosphere, the crunch of dead leaves the only sound as he trod until... 'That's it.' Ben quickened his step and emerged out of the trees onto a clearing that sloped gently down to the edge of a cliff and the vast blue waters of the Pacific Ocean beyond. Shading his eyes from the sun, he scoured the tree line that bordered the clearing and tried to think in which direction Ivy Cottage lay. As he did so, he heard the tinkling of a bell. Strangely, it awoke something deep inside. He followed the sound, stumbling over the terrain as he went, until the peak of a roof came into view as if hovering above the trees. He hastened his step and pushed his way forward into the undergrowth until he found himself at the eroded edge of the cliff. High above, seagulls soared and in the face of a cool nor-easterly wind, he looked down to where the sheer wall of the cliff, wet with salt spray, gleamed in the afternoon sun above rocks in the churning sea. The image of his mother's body splayed on the rocks flashed in front of him and he lurched back from the edge. Shaking, he turned to see the small clapboard structure that had once been her studio. With so many years of neglect, the cottage now lay hidden in the dense vegetation, virtually invisible to the naked eye. Above the doorway, its name, "Ivy Cottage", hung precariously from one remaining nail. Beside it, a rusty metal mobile full of tiny bells, tinkled with the wind. The door of the cottage stood ajar. Surprised, he opened the door further and hesitantly peered inside. As he did so, the hairs on the back of his neck stood on end and a sense of foreboding gripped him. Pushing the feeling away, he crossed the threshold.

Untouched since the day Rachael Carmichael plunged to her death, the room remained as she had left it as if waiting for her return. Her easel stood in the centre of the room in the light of the front window, an unfinished painting perched there in anticipation of her next brush stroke. Beneath the easel, a photograph lay in the midst of shards of glass and a mangled silver frame. Ben knelt down, wiped away the glass and tentatively picked the photograph up. Faded with time the long forgotten image of his mother looked out at him. Beside her, in an awkward stance, stood a small boy, squinting in the sunlight. In her arms a baby. 'Joanna,' he said quietly to himself. Ben studied his mother's smiling face and a lump formed in his throat. The striking resemblance of the small boy to the woman in the photograph was not lost on him.

Clutching the photograph and despite his sense of disquiet when he first entered the cottage, he continued on, each room producing a hint of déjà vu. Ultimately, with his curiosity satisfied, he retraced his steps and headed for the front door. As he did so, however, he heard a sound and looked back. The cottage resumed its silence. It was then his gaze fell upon a large tapestry hung against the far wall. Puzzled by its presence, he tried to picture the room as he remembered it. There was no tapestry, he thought to himself. He walked over and reached out to touch it. All at once, Ben ripped the tapestry aside to see a door, slightly ajar. It creaked as he opened it further. With its window covered in ivy the room lay in darkness. Hesitantly, he stepped inside and as he did, he fell forward. 'What the hell!' he barked. When he fumbled for his torch, its light revealed a body.

CHAPTER 11

Fitzjohn rose at first light, donned a pair of old beige shorts, a faded green shirt, and made his way downstairs. As he did so, a snore came from the guest bedroom, indicating that his sister, Meg, still slept. With relief, he smiled to himself and descended the stairs happy in the knowledge that he could follow his usual morning routine unhindered. In the kitchen, he grabbed the container of bird seed, slipped his feet into his gardening shoes, and opened the back door. Outside, he breathed in the fresh morning air and sighed, surveying the flower beds, their blooms a mass of colour. At the birdfeeder hung in the jacaranda tree, rainbow lorikeets squawked and fluttered in an effort to wrangle their positions in the line-up. Fitzjohn watched the foray with amusement. 'Even you lot have a pecking order,' he muttered to himself, pouring seed into the dish. The parrots dived for it and Fitzjohn continued on to the greenhouse, the orchids inside hidden behind the misted windows. Opening the door, he turned on the CD player, and the soft sound of

Mozart's Clarinet Concerto in A Major filled the air. Time slipped by unnoticed whilst he made his way along the rows of plants, tending to each one in turn.

'Alistair. Are you in there, Alistair?'

Brought back from his musings, Fitzjohn looked at his watch and frowned before opening the door to find Meg, wrapped in her dressing gown. 'I don't know where the time's gone. Thanks for coming down to remind me, Meg,' he said, stepping outside and closing the greenhouse door behind him.

'I'm not out here to remind you about the time, Alistair. I need to talk to you about Sophie, *before* you leave for work.'

'It'll have to wait until this evening,' replied Fitzjohn, starting toward the house. 'I don't have time now. Betts will be here soon to pick me up.'

Meg bustled after him. 'But this can't wait. You have to help me persuade Sophie to stop all this nonsense and return to Melbourne where she belongs.'

Fitzjohn turned to face his sister. 'Meg, I know your heart's in the right place, but Sophie's no longer a child. You can't tell her what to do or where to live. Not anymore.'

Meg gaped at Fitzjohn. 'I knew it. I just knew it. You two are in collaboration, aren't you? I'd never have let that girl come to Sydney if I'd known you'd not back me up. This is too much, Alistair. Just *too* much.'

'I'm sorry you feel that way, Meg.' Fitzjohn touched his sister's arm. 'We'll talk further this evening. I promise.'

Meg shrugged Fitzjohn's hand off her arm and flounced through the back door and into the house.

Now dressed in a dark grey suit and blue tie against a crisp white shirt, Fitzjohn made his way downstairs and into the kitchen where he found Betts and Meg in conversation. 'Good morning Betts,' he sang out.

'Morning, sir.'

Meg gave Fitzjohn a frosty look.

'As I said, Meg. We'll talk this evening.' Meg turned away and busied herself at the kitchen sink. Fitzjohn raised his eyebrows, turned and closed his briefcase. 'See you this evening.' Followed by Betts, he started toward the front door.

Silence prevailed as the two men settled themselves into the car before Fitzjohn handed Betts Sophie's green plastic bag. 'I believe this contains something of yours.'

'It does?' Betts opened the bag and peered inside. 'Oh. It's my sweater. How did you get it?' Betts looked into Fitzjohn's piercing stare. 'I can explain, sir.'

Fitzjohn pulled his seat belt on. 'I thought I'd made myself clear as far as my niece is concerned, Betts. She's off limits. You're far too old for her.'

'I'm not that old, sir.'

'You are as far as Sophie is concerned.' Fitzjohn pursed his lips.

Betts scratched his ear. 'Mmm. I suppose I am a bit. It's just that Sophie asked me to help her move into her new apartment. How could I refuse?'

'Politely,' replied Fitzjohn. 'Now, to business. 'Any news on Van Goren?'

'No, sir, but I do have the Coroner's report into the Rachael Carmichael death.' Betts handed the report to Fitzjohn. 'She died in September, 1983, after falling from a cliff top that borders the property at Whale Beach. The property Theodora Hunt told us about. It's called Lane's End.'

'So, what caused her to fall?'

'The coroner's findings were inconclusive,' continued Betts. 'It couldn't be proved whether it was an accident, suicide or if foul play was involved.' Fitzjohn leafed through the report as Betts turned the ignition and pulled away from the curb.

'Did she have a history of depression?' asked Fitzjohn.

'Not as far as any records show.'

Fitzjohn sat in thought before he said, 'Very well. In that case, I'd like to look at the investigation records into her death. Find out who the investigating officer in charge of the case was at the time, will you, Betts?'

'I already have, sir.'

'Good. Who is it?'

Betts scratched the back of his neck.

'Well?' said Fitzjohn.

'It was Chief Superintendent Grieg, sir.'

Fitzjohn gaped at Betts.

'Then a Detective Senior Sergeant.' Betts gave Fitzjohn a wry smile and chuckled. 'Could be interesting. You questioning the Chief Superintendent about his *unsolved* case.'

'Interesting indeed.' Fitzjohn's thoughts went to Grieg's outburst the day before when he had learnt of his involvement in the Carmichael case. Could that be the reason Grieg had not wanted him on the case? Because of his, apparent, unsolved case?

'There's something else, sir. Not related to our case, of course, but I'm sure you'll be pleased to hear that Ben Carmichael's fiancée, Emma Phillips, has been found.'

'Well! That is good news. Is she okay?'

'She's alive, but in a coma. Apparently medically induced. It's not yet known what happened to her.'

Fitzjohn's brow furrowed. 'Where was she found?'

'At Lane's End by Ben Carmichael. According to the police officer who attended, Mr Carmichael was in the process of retracing Emma's steps since her disappearance. He'd found out that she had asked Laura Carmichael for permission to visit the Lane's End property to do some research for a book she's writing. The reason being that Emma wanted to include Rachael Carmichael in that book. According to Ben Carmichael, that permission hadn't been granted, but he thought she might have gone there anyway. He found her in the cottage that Rachael used as a studio.'

'I see.' Fitzjohn fell into silence as he looked down at the Coroner's Report and began to read. When their car arrived at Day Street Police Station, he closed the report and said, 'I'd like to go to Lane's End, Betts. Make the arrangements, will you?'

Fitzjohn and Betts arrived at Lane's End later that same day to find police cars lined up along the lane-way and a young constable at the entrance. 'It looks pretty run down,' said Betts, peering through the car window and beyond the stone wall into the grounds.

'Not surprising after so many years of abandonment,' replied Fitzjohn, opening the car door and climbing out.

After showing their warrant cards to the constable on duty, they made their way along the winding driveway, its gravel scattered into the foliage. 'It must have been a beautiful place at one time,' said Fitzjohn, his gaze taking in the geometric lines of old flower beds now overgrown with weeds. As they rounded the bend in the drive, a derelict two-storey stone house came into view. Another police officer stood nearby.

'Good afternoon, Constable,' said Fitzjohn, holding up his warrant card once again. 'I'm DCI Fitzjohn and this is DS Betts. We're from Sydney City LAC. We're here to speak to DCI Roberts.'

'He's expecting you, sir, although he's some distance away at the other side of the property. If you'll come this way.'

'Fitzjohn and Betts followed the constable along a narrow path that ran beside the house and passed another, smaller stone dwelling before entering dense bushland.

'You'll have to watch your step in here, sir,' said the Constable. 'I've seen the odd snake.' Betts looked disconcertedly at Fitzjohn before he tripped over a tree root.

'It would've been impossible to get an ambulance in here,' said Fitzjohn, looking up, the sky all but obscured by foliage.

'The young lady was carried out on a stretcher, sir,' replied the Constable.

They reached the edge of the tree-line and emerged out into a clearing where a number of officers stood. One of them, a man in his mid-fifties, broke away from the group when Fitzjohn and Betts approached.

'Alistair,' he said, making his way toward them. 'It's been a while.'

'It has, David. Good to see you. This is my sergeant, Martin Betts.' Fitzjohn half turned toward Betts.

David Roberts nodded before he said, 'When we spoke, you said you're working on a case that's related, in some way, to the young woman who was found here. The homicide at the Observatory isn't it?'

'That's right. She's the fiancée of Ben Carmichael. His father, Richard, was a host at the cocktail party held at the Observatory that night. And this property is owned by the Carmichael family.'

'Ah. I see.'

'Where was Emma Phillips found, David?'

'In a cottage on the other side of this clearing. Come, I'll show you.' They followed Roberts to a small building all but hidden in the vegetation, its frontage facing the sea. 'It seems the young woman was left here to die a lonely death.' Roberts led the way inside to where the SOCO's worked.

'So, you don't think it was an accident,' said Fitzjohn, casting his eye around the front room.

'No. She'd been bludgeoned and left in the adjoining room over there.' Roberts gestured to an open doorway on the far wall. 'According to her fiancé, Ben Carmichael, the entrance was covered up by that tapestry we have bagged up over there. He just happened to remember that there'd been a doorway on that wall.' Roberts shook his head. 'Just as well, otherwise it would have been too late. God only knows how long it would have been before she was discovered. By the look of the property, it doesn't look like it's been used in years.'

'It hasn't,' said Fitzjohn, peering at the painting that sat on the easel. 'Thirty years to be exact. There was a death here in 1983. A woman by the name of Rachael Carmichael. She was an artist and, I'm told, used this cottage as her studio.'

David Roberts looked thoughtful. 'I remember that. She fell from the cliff, didn't she?' Fitzjohn nodded. 'She must have been the woman in the photograph Mr Carmichael found and also on the remnants of another, torn up and scattered across the floor where Emma Phillips lay.'

'Sounds disturbing,' said Fitzjohn.

'It does.'

'Have you found a weapon,' asked Fitzjohn.

'No, but we have located the young lady's car hidden in some bushes behind the house at the front of the property.'

With the heat in the cottage building, Fitzjohn took his handkerchief from his breast pocket and dabbed his forehead before they made their way outside. There, in the face of a cooling sea breeze, he walked to the edge of the cliff and looked down to the rocks below. They walked in silence for a time back through the property to their car, Fitzjohn smoothing down the few remaining wisps of hair left on top of his head as he went. 'Of course, there is sort of a family connection between Emma Phillips and Rachael Carmichael through Emma's engagement to Ben Carmichael,' he said at last. 'But I wonder if that connection extends to this attack on Emma and the death of Rachael?'

'You've lost me, sir,' replied Betts as they made their way out of Lane's End to their car.

'Well, it's just that Emma Phillips was conducting research into Rachael Carmichael's artistic life for a book on artists, wasn't she?'

'That's right,' replied Betts.

'So, as part of her research, Emma came here to the place where Rachael had worked and died. I think there's every chance that she stumbled upon something to do with Rachael's death. What hospital did DCI Roberts say Ms Phillips was taken to?'

'North Shore, sir.'

'Mmm. The same hospital that Richard Carmichael died in only days ago. It can't have been easy for his son to return there so soon,' replied Fitzjohn thoughtfully.

Fitzjohn and Betts arrived at North Shore Hospital and made their way to the Intensive Care Unit. There they found Ben Carmichael pacing the floor outside the unit. 'Mr Carmichael,' said Fitzjohn, walking toward him. Ben, his face ragged and drawn, stopped pacing and looked toward the two officers. 'We understand your fiancée has been found.'

'Yes, thank God. I found her this morning at Lane's End.'

'And how is she?'

'I'm not sure.' Ben shook his head. 'The doctors have put her in a medically induced coma. They said it would be just until the swelling in her brain recedes, although I'm told that there's no telling how long it could take before she's conscious again.'

'And no way of knowing who attacked her,' said Fitzjohn. Ben shook his head. 'In that case, we'll leave what we want to talk to you about until another time, Mr Carmichael. Perhaps tomorrow if things improve for Emma.'

'Tomorrow's my father's funeral, Chief Inspector.' Ben ran his hand through his dark wavy hair. 'If you have more questions about Peter Van Goren, I don't think I can tell you any more than I already have. I honestly didn't know the man.'

'It isn't Mr Van Goren we want to ask you about, Mr Carmichael. It's about Emma,' replied Fitzjohn.

'Oh? I was under the impression another police officer was handling that case. Roberts I think he said his name is.'

'That's correct. DCI Roberts is in charge of Emma's case. However, we wondered if you might be able to identify the people in a photograph that was found on the floor where Emma was found.'

'I didn't notice a photo there, but then the room was in darkness.'

'It'd been torn in pieces and scattered.' Fitzjohn looked to Betts who brought a photograph, encased in a plastic sleeve, out from a folder he held. He handed it to Ben. 'It's been pieced together and as you can see, some of the faces aren't clear. Even so, we hoped you might have some idea who the people are.'

Ben Carmichael stared at the image in silence before he said, 'It's a photograph of Joanna and me with our mother. I found a similar one in the cottage on the floor under the easel. Its frame had been shattered and it looked like someone had ground the photo into the floor with the heel of their shoe.'

'Do you know who the other people in this photo are?' asked Fitzjohn.

Ben studied the image again. 'The face of the woman next to my mother looks like the woman who used to be our housekeeper. Amanda Marsh is her name.'

'Amanda Marsh?' said Fitzjohn. 'We met a woman by that name at the Observatory the night Peter Van Goren died.'

'Yes, you would have. Apparently, after my mother's death, Amanda moved on and started her own catering business.'

'I see. So, she's remained in touch with your family?' replied Fitzjohn.

'Only in as far as catering for functions held by Carmichael Hunt Real Estate.'

'What about the man in the photograph standing next to Ms Marsh?' asked Fitzjohn. I know his image is far from clear, but do you have any idea who he might be?'

'Well, he's not tall enough to be my uncle, Sebastian Newberry, or my father, for that matter.' Ben shook his head. 'I'm sorry, Chief Inspector. I don't know who he is.' Ben handed the photograph back to Betts.

———

'Right,' said Fitzjohn as he and Betts left the hospital. 'Tomorrow I want to talk to Amanda Marsh again because it seems she had more to do with the Carmichael family than providing her catering services.

CHAPTER 12

Those who gathered at Richard Carmichael's graveside did so in silence, the mourners who had attended the cocktail party only days before still reeling in the knowledge that Richard was now dead. Ben and Joanna stood on either side of Laura, her face expressionless, both hands clasped together in front of her. Emerson Hunt and his wife, Theodora, together with Sebastian Newberry, positioned themselves on the other side of the casket. Ben's gaze came to rest on Emerson, who fidgeted with the signet ring on his right hand. Theodora stemmed her tears with a tissue. Sebastian cast his eyes down. Behind him, Amanda Marsh looked straight ahead from beneath her large-brimmed black hat.

When the minister's words came to an end and those assembled dispersed, Ben and Joanna waited while Laura spoke to Theodora and Emerson Hunt.

'The police are here,' said Joanna, looking toward Fitzjohn and Betts who could be seen on a grass verge some distance away. 'Why, I wonder?' As Joanna spoke, the two officers turned and walked to their car.

'I'm not sure,' replied Ben. 'But if you think about it, it's likely that the person who killed Peter Van Goren is here among us.'

'Oh.' Joanna grimaced and looked around at the mourners now walking away from the graveside toward their cars. 'I suppose you're right. And whoever that person is, is about to make his way to Mosman to offer condolences and sip Earl Grey tea with us.'

'What makes you think it's a man, Joanna?'

A look of shock came to Joanna's face. 'Well, it couldn't be a woman. Could it?' Ben shrugged.

'Thanks for waiting, you two,' said Laura as she approached and they started towards their car. 'I just wanted to thank Theodora and Emerson. They've been so kind to me over the past few days.' Ben opened the car door. 'Was that the police I saw earlier?' Laura continued.

'Yes,' replied Ben.

'Then they must think that someone at the funeral killed Mr Van Goren.' Laura sighed. 'Oh dear.'

—————

Guests were already congregating at the Carmichael residence when Laura, along with Ben and Joanna, arrived. Ben looked at the strained face of his step-mother. 'Are you okay, Laura?'

'Yes, I'm fine.' She tapped his arm and walked into the house and through to the living room to greet the guests.

In the front hall, Ben and Joanna received the continual flow of mourners, amongst them Theodora, followed by Emerson. With her tight black dress accentuating her plump shape, and her long blonde curls swept up and held by a butterfly-shaped hat, Theodora took each of their hands. 'Darlings, we know how devastated you both must be. Don't we, Emerson?' she said, shooting a look his way. 'And you especially Ben, with Emma still in the hospital. How is she, dear?'

'Only time will tell, Theodora.' Ben gave a quick smile and removed his hand from her tight grasp. 'We'll have to wait and see.'

'Of course you will, but remember, if there's anything we can do, you have only to ask.'

'Thank you both,' replied Ben as he shook Emerson's hand. 'Please, go through.'

Emerson ushered Theodora into the living room and Ben followed soon after, leaving Joanna to greet the remaining mourners. As he did so, he glimpsed Amanda Marsh walking toward him. He had little memory of her time as his parents' housekeeper and was always puzzled at her familiarity on the rare occasions that they had met.

'Ben. It's been a long time,' she said, taking hold of his arm, her face full of concern. 'I'm so sorry about your father. So sudden. It makes it doubly hard, I know.' Amanda shook her head. 'You and Joanna will have to help your stepmother through her grief. Oh, there she is now, the poor dear.' Amanda put her hand out to Laura as she walked past. 'Mrs Carmichael, may I offer my condolences. Richard will be sadly missed.'

'He will, Ms Marsh,' replied Laura, a certain tension evident as she faced Amanda. 'Thank you for attending today. I know how busy you are.' As she spoke another guest caught Laura's eye and she excused herself with what Ben thought a great deal of grace.

'A difficult day for her,' continued Amanda, turning back to Ben. 'And for you too, of course. I heard on the news about your fiancée's ordeal. How is she, Ben?'

'She's making progress slowly,' he replied, following DCI Roberts's advice not to go into detail about Emma's situation.

'I'm glad to hear it.'

'It's been a difficult week for you also,' he continued, wishing to change the subject.

'It certainly has. Not only was I catering for your father's cocktail party last Friday night, but I was the person who found the body!'

Ben grimaced. 'That must have been upsetting for you.'

'Chilling to say the least. I haven't been able to sleep since.' Amanda took a sip of her white wine before she looked around the room. 'And now this. Who would have thought...?'

When the last of the guests had left, Laura came back into the living room and sat down heavily into an armchair. 'Well, I'm glad that's over. I found it difficult knowing it's conceivable that one of the mourners likely killed Peter Van Goren.' She sighed and looked to Ben and Joanna. 'Thanks you two for your help and support. I couldn't have got through this day without you both. And I know it's especially difficult for you, Ben, with Emma in the hospital.' Silence ensued until Laura continued. 'Look, I know it's the last thing you both want to hear right now, but I want to read your father's will.'

'Are you sure?' asked Ben. 'Wouldn't you sooner leave it for another day? After all, it won't be an easy task.'

'I know, but as your father's executrix, it's one of my duties and I think the sooner I get it over with, the better.' Laura rose from her chair and went to the writing desk that sat in the corner of the room. From it she took a long narrow envelope and sat down again before putting her reading glasses on. After reading through the preliminaries, she looked over her glasses at Joanna. 'Joanna, your Dad wanted you to have the house that you've been renting from him for the past two years. There's also a bequest of $100,000 that you'll receive through his solicitors, Murray, Bennett, Walker.' Laura turned to the third page of the will. 'And to you, Ben, your father has bequeathed Lane's End at Whale Beach.'

Ben sat forward in his chair. 'Lane's End? But I thought... that is, I thought Dad would want the property sold after his death.'

'I thought so too before I read through the will last night, so I was as surprised as you are now. We all know he couldn't bring himself to sell the place while he lived. It seems he can't in death either.' Laura frowned. 'I could never understand it. It was as if he was trapped. Not able to bring himself to return to Lane's End or let anyone else for that matter.' Laura removed her reading glasses. 'It's a shame, really, because I think we have to face the past in order to move on. Anyway, Ben, Lane's End is now yours to do with as you wish. All the papers are in your father's study and you're welcome to go through them whenever you like.' Laura looked down once again at the pages of the will. 'It seems the remainder of the estate has been left to me.' She placed the will back into its envelope and rested it on the arm of the chair.

———

Later that day, with the last shaft of afternoon sun caressing the room, Ben walked into the study. Dominated by a large oak desk, its walls lined with shelves of books, it exuded an atmosphere of hard work and success. Not since the day he had walked away from a promising career in academia had Ben set foot inside the room. That day the gulf that had always existed between him and his father grew wider, and only ended in death. The words they had spoken now echoed through Ben's mind. Recriminations that fed the bitterness to come. Young and ambitious, he had felt no guilt at his father's disappointment in him even though, at the time, he had little idea of what he wanted to do with his life. All he knew was he loathed the path he was on. Living his father's vision for him. A career in astrophysics. Ben pulled the leather chair out from the desk and sat down. In front of him sat all the papers in connection with Lane's End. At that moment, Joanna walked in.

'What will you do? Sell it?' she asked, perching on the arm of the chair in the corner of the room.

Ben sat back. 'I'm not sure. It's not something I thought I'd ever have to decide on. I'll have to think about it, although, after finding Emma there like I did, and the fact our mother died there, I'm not sure I want to keep the place.'

Joanna slid from the arm into the chair. 'Well, if you want my opinion, it might be just as well to sell. Get rid of the past once and for all.' Joanna sighed. 'I don't know about you, Ben, but it's always been like an albatross around my neck. All my life. Lane's End was there, but never mentioned. It's as if our mother was never put to rest. Not really.'

'Mmm. I know what you mean. In fact everything, her untimely death, Dad's passing away, Emma in the hospital in an induced coma... it's surreal. Although I do think I now understand one thing out of all this, and that is, why my relationship with Dad never worked.'

'Oh? Why?'

'Because of this.' Ben took a photograph from his inner suit pocket and handed it to his sister. 'It's a picture of us both with our mother when we were children. I'd have shown it to you earlier but the police had it.'

Joanna scrutinised the image, a soft smile on her face. 'She beautiful, isn't she? And there I am in her arms. And you beside her.' Joanna looked up at Ben. 'You look so much like her, Ben. It's uncanny.' Joanna's eyes grew wide. 'Oh. I see what you mean. You think you reminded Dad of her. Every day.' Joanna paused. 'He did love you, though. You do know that, don't you? He just found everything to do with our mother very difficult to deal with.'

They sat for a time in silence before Joanna said, 'I don't like to bring it up at a time like this, Ben, but did you contact that solicitor who wrote to you?'

'No. Whatever it is, it'll have to wait.'

'I don't think it can wait,' replied Joanna. 'After all, it's about a man who has been murdered. A man who has named you in his will. Don't you see, it connects you to Peter Van Goren. You need to find out what it's all about because if you don't, I think the police will, eventually.' Joanna paused. 'I can sit with Emma while you go to see Raymond West.'

———

Under a threatening sky and the sound of thunder in the distance, Ben made his way by train to Wynyard Station in Sydney's CBD where he emerged onto George Street. With a light rain falling, he pressed the button on his umbrella and watched it unfurl before he stepped out into the hubbub of the city. He went by way of Martin Place and as he walked along the wide pedestrian mall to Phillip Street, he found the opportunity to reflect on the contents of the solicitor's letter, and tried to put the events of the last forty-eight hours into some kind of perspective.

He arrived at the building that housed West Longmire & Associates, still unsure of his response to the fact that he had been named as a beneficiary in Peter Van Goren's will. Joining a number of others in the elevator, he emerged onto the 2nd level where he opened the glass doors of the solicitor's office into a reception area. A woman in her mid-fifties with short dark wavy hair, sat behind a desk. She looked up when Ben approached. As she did so, the sound of raised voices came from an inner office.

'Good afternoon,' she said with a quick nervous smile, her eyes darting sideways toward the voices. 'Can I help you?'

'Yes. I have an appointment with Mr West at two o'clock.' Ben smiled.

The receptionist looked at her computer screen. 'Mr Carmichael, is it?' she asked, distracted by the commotion. 'Yes. Ben Carmichael.'

'Please take a seat, Mr Carmichael. Mr West will be with you shortly.' She gave another quick smile.

Ben sat down in one of the chairs lined up along the wall of the reception area and flicked through a BRW magazine whereupon a woman emerged from an inner office, followed by a stout man in his late forties.

'I expect better things of you, Mr West,' she barked. 'If you can't settle this matter in my favour, say so, and I'll find another solicitor.'

With his colour rising in embarrassment, Raymond West stood in silence as the woman flounced out of the office. At that point he adjusted his heavy-rimmed glasses and turned toward Ben. 'Mr Carmichael?'

'Yes,' replied Ben, impressed by the solicitor's quick recovery.

'I'm Raymond West. You must feel like my next victim.' He gave Ben a wry smile. 'Won't you come this way?' Towering over West, Ben followed the solicitor past the receptionist and along the hall into a small office, its atmosphere lending a nostalgic feel. 'Please, make yourself comfortable,' he said.

Ben sat down in one of the chairs offered while West settled himself at his desk and opened the file in front of him.

'Thank you for coming in to see me, Mr Carmichael,' he said, clasping his hands together. 'I'm sorry that your introduction to our legal practice turned out to be somewhat soap operatic. Still, such occurrences do keep one's day from becoming dull.' Raymond West smiled. 'Now, to your matter.

As I mentioned in my letter, you've been named as a beneficiary in the last will and testament of my client, Peter Van Goren.' West unclasped his hands and looked down at the file. 'In fact, other than bequests to Mr Van Goren's household staff, you are his sole beneficiary.'

'Mr West, before we proceed, are you aware that I didn't know Peter Van Goren?' asked Ben with a measure of concern. 'I'm sure you have the wrong Ben Carmichael.'

West looked at Ben over his glasses.

'According to my instructions, Mr Carmichael, I can assure you that you are the Benjamin Carmichael that Peter Van Goren named as his beneficiary, but if it will make you feel more comfortable, I can read you the details, about yourself, that Peter Van Goren furnished me with.' Raymond West shuffled through the file and brought out a sheet of paper. 'Now, let me see,' he said, peering through his bifocals. 'Your full name is Benjamin Richard Carmichael, the son of Richard and Rachael Carmichael. You were born on the 17th of May, 1977, educated at Shore, Sydney Church of England Grammar School, and later at The University of Sydney. There, you obtained a Bachelor of Astrophysics with Honours. And,' West's brow furrowed. 'You are a photojournalist by occupation.' West gave Ben a quizzical look.

'You're thinking that it's an unlikely career choice after studying astrophysics,' said Ben.

West chuckled. 'It did cross my mind. I might have liked to do the same thing after law school, but it would have killed my father.' West paused, as if to reflect for a moment. 'Anyway, Mr Carmichael, have I managed to allay your fears about your eligibility as Peter Van Goren's beneficiary?' Ben nodded. 'Good, then I'll now read out Mr Van Goren's last will and testament.'

Ben listened as Raymond West read the opening paragraph of the will before reading out the bequests to Peter Van Goren's staff.

'"To my housekeeper, Ida Clegg, I leave the sum of three hundred thousand dollars and my home at number two, Wentworth Street, Vaucluse, New South Wales. To my other household staff, Marjorie Reynolds, my cook, and Leonard Preston, groundsman and chauffeur, I leave the sum of two hundred thousand dollars each. The remainder of my estate, I leave to Benjamin Richard Carmichael. This includes all monies, shares, debenture stocks, and my business interests as listed below."'

When Raymond West finished, he removed his glasses and sat back. 'I don't need to tell you, Mr Carmichael, it's a considerable sum.'

'I don't know what to say,' replied Ben. 'I feel uncomfortable being a beneficiary of someone I didn't know, but this makes it... Are you sure Mr Van Goren had no family?'

'That was one of the first questions I asked him when he made this will,' replied West. 'Because as you may or may not be aware, any children of a deceased can contest a will that leaves them nothing. Mr Van Goren, however, assured me that he did not have any off-spring nor did he have any next-of-kin.'

'Can I ask how long Mr Van Goren had been your client, Mr West?' asked Ben.

'I've taken instruction from Peter Van Goren for many years. He first came to see me in the 1980s when he purchased his first commercial property, and then again for the conveyance of his home in Vaucluse.'

Still bewildered by Raymond West's insistence that he was the right beneficiary, Ben left the city and made his way to the hospital, where Joanna waited.

'Has there been any change?' he whispered as he joined her at Emma's bedside.

'No.' Joanna got up from her chair and looked back down at Emma's still form. 'She looks like she's sleeping peacefully, doesn't she?'

Ben stroked Emma's hand that lay on top of the covers. 'I hope she eventually wakes up,' replied Ben, only too aware that there was a chance she may not.

'She will,' said Joanna, following Ben from the ICU. 'You have to believe she will.'

They made their way along the corridor to the small waiting room and sat down. 'What did the solicitor have to say? Did you tell him that you didn't know Mr Van Goren?'

'Yes. I questioned him as to whether he had the right Ben Carmichael and he's adamant he does. He went through a list of details that Peter Van Goren had given him about me. They're all correct.' Ben looked at his sister. 'I can't understand it, Joanna. I really can't. As you know, I've never met Peter Van Goren. To make me his sole beneficiary is ridiculous.'

'Sole beneficiary?'

'Yes. Other than bequests to three members of his staff, Mr Van Goren left me his entire estate. As I said before, this whole situation is surreal.'

'What are you going to do?' asked Joanna, looking puzzled.

'I don't know.' Ben leaned back in his chair and rubbed his face with his hands.

'Well, I think you should start by telling that detective who's investigating Peter Van Goren's death. Surely under the circumstances, the police will want to know.'

'I imagine they already do know and unfortunately, it won't look good as far as Dad is concerned.'

'Why? Dad wouldn't have known what Mr Van Goren's will contained.'

'Perhaps not, but with Peter Van Goren making me his sole beneficiary, they're bound to think he and Dad knew each other and surmise that Dad knew about the will. Don't you see, Joanna? In their eyes, it gives Dad a motive to kill Mr Van Goren.'

☞ CHAPTER 13 ☜

'Can I give you a lift home, sir?' asked Betts, putting his head around the side of Fitzjohn's office door.

Fitzjohn looked up at his young sergeant, a tinge of guilt surfacing after the reprimand he had given him over Sophie. 'Thanks, Betts, but I want to read through this Investigation Report into Rachael Carmichael's death again and also speak to Chief Superintendent Grieg before I leave this evening. It'll help to have his thoughts on the case before we talk to Amanda Marsh in the morning.'

Once Betts left, Fitzjohn settled back in his chair and began to read the report before he stopped. Was his concern for Sophie's welfare merely interference, something that he did not like to see his sister, Meg, do. Fitzjohn sighed and went back to the report. When he had finished, he pulled his suit coat on, straightened his tie, and made his way through the station to Grieg's office. He knocked once and put his head around the side of the door to find the Chief Superintendent sat hunched over at his desk.

'What is it?' grunted Grieg.

'I'd like to speak to you about an old case,' replied Fitzjohn, stepping inside.

'Oh? What case is that? And why?'

'It was an investigation into the death of a woman by the name of Rachael Carmichael in September, 1983. And the reason I want to speak to you about it is because as I'm sure you're aware, the Carmichael family happen to be involved in my present investigation.'

Grieg glared at Fitzjohn, his manner exuding his arrogant nature. 'Why come to me?' he sneered. 'I think you'll find that that investigation was conducted by our now retired Chief Superintendent Fellowes. He was a Detective Chief Inspector at the time. So, you're wrong, Fitzjohn. It wasn't me.'

'I agree, he was in charge initially, sir, but according to the records, only up until he was taken ill. At which time you took charge.' Fitzjohn gave a quick smile. 'It's probably slipped your memory. After all, it was a *long* time ago.'

Grieg's eyes narrowed at Fitzjohn. 'Okay,' he said, sitting back and throwing his pen onto the desk. 'What do you want to know?'

'I had hoped you could give me your thoughts on the case, sir.'

Grieg bristled. 'I can't see what possible difference my thoughts on an old case can have on your present one.'

'Oh, but I'm sure it will,' replied Fitzjohn. 'A bit of added insight into the Carmichael family can only help.'

'Well, I don't see how because there's little to tell. There were no witnesses as to what really happened to Rachael Carmichael. She'd gone out early that morning to paint, leaving her two young children with the housekeeper. She wasn't discovered missing until mid-afternoon when her brother-in-law arrived from the city and went to seek her out.'

'The investigation report mentions a gardener who absconded on that day, sir.'

'That's right. Everything led to the fact that he was responsible for Mrs Carmichael's death, but we couldn't question him because he was never found.'

'So it was left at that?' asked Fitzjohn, frowning.

Grieg shrugged. 'There was nothing else to be done with the situation as it was, Fitzjohn. We didn't have the manpower to spend any more time on the case when everything pointed to the gardener. Plus the fact that the Coroner's Court couldn't prove that there was foul play involved. Rachael Carmichael's death might have been suicide or an accident.' Grieg sat forward again, grabbed his pen and looked at Fitzjohn dismissively. 'Now, if you'll excuse me.'

So, thought Fitzjohn, smiling to himself as he left Grieg's office. That's why Grieg didn't want me on the Carmichael case. He knew I'd find out about his *unsolved* case. Back in his own office, Fitzjohn picked up the telephone and dialed Reginald Fellowes's number.

———

As the shadows of the city skyscrapers lengthened with the setting sun, Fitzjohn left the station and made his way out to the waiting car. After placing his briefcase on the back seat, he opened the passenger door to find Williams at the wheel.

'Evening, sir.'

'Good evening, Williams.' As he spoke, Fitzjohn thought again as to whether Williams had been Grieg's mole at Kings Cross LAC. Perhaps this evening was one way to find out.

'Where to, sir? Home?'

'Yes, but first I want to go to Frenchs Forest to see our retired Chief Superintendent, Reginald Fellowes.'

'Oh. So, you two keep in touch then, sir.' Williams pulled the car away from the kerb. 'That's a good thing because it can't be easy to retire and have no contact with those you've served with for so many years.' Williams paused. 'I hope there's someone who still wants to see me after I retire.'

'I'm sure there will be, Williams. This, however, isn't a social call.' They continued on in silence. If Williams was, indeed, Grieg's mole, thought Fitzjohn, no doubt Grieg would hear of his visit to see Reginald by first thing the next morning.

———

The door opened to reveal a tall man of large proportions with a shock of thick white hair, his quiet, determined nature still evident. 'Alistair,' he said with a broad smile. 'It's good to see you. Come in.'

'Sorry for the late hour, Reg,' replied Fitzjohn, stepping inside and following Fellowes into the living room.

'Not a problem. I welcome the company.' Fellowes gestured to one of the armchairs. 'I was just having a whisky. Would you like one? I brought back a nice drop from Scotland last month while on holiday.'

'Thanks,' replied Fitzjohn, sitting down.

Fellowes handed Fitzjohn a glass before he sat down himself. 'You said on the phone you wanted to ask me about an old case I was involved in.'

'That's right. It was the investigation into the death of a woman by the name of Rachael Carmichael at a place called Lane's End in September, 1983.'

'Rachael Carmichael?' Fellowes thought for a moment. 'Ah, yes. I do remember it. She fell from a cliff up on the northern beaches. Why are you interested?' Fellowes took a sip of his drink.

'Because my present case into the murder of a man at the Observatory last Friday night involves Rachael Carmichael's family.'

'Ah. You're on that case, are you?' said Fellowes. 'I read about it in the newspaper. Some chap with a foreign sounding name died. Van something.'

'Van Goren. Peter Van Goren,' replied Fitzjohn. 'He'd attended a function held by Rachael Carmichael's husband, Richard.'

'Now I'm with you.' Fellowes paused. 'I met Richard Carmichael, of course, when his wife died. Seemed like a nice chap as I remember. How do you think I can help, Alistair?'

'I hope you can give me your thoughts on what happened to Rachael because after reading through the Coroner's Report, it seems there was no conclusion as to how she died.'

'That's right,' said Fellowes. 'But I doubt I can help because I wasn't on the case for very long. I got sick that winter and had to surrender it to another officer, a Senior Sergeant at the time, who is, by the way, the now Chief Superintendent Grieg.'

'So I understand.'

'Have you spoken to him about the case?' asked Fellowes.

'I have, but without much success.'

'Mmm. I don't wonder. I seem to remember that Evelyn wasn't at all pleased about being seconded to take on that case in the first place.'

'Evelyn?' Fitzjohn's brow furrowed.

'Yes. Evelyn Grieg. He once told me his mother had named him after Evelyn Waugh, the English writer. Didn't you know?'

'No,' replied Fitzjohn, amused. 'I've never seen his given name on any paperwork. And you say that, at the time, he was seconded to Day Street Station. From where?'

'North Shore LAC, and, as it turned out, it was a one-way move.' Fellowes's right eyebrow arched. 'It was obvious they didn't want him back. I think that fact has stuck in his craw ever since. I doubt he wants to be reminded by questions about the case that brought him to Day Street in the first place, let alone that it was never solved. I wouldn't expect too much cooperation if I were you.'

'I never do,' replied Fitzjohn. He sipped his whisky. 'I've read the investigation report. By all accounts, it was thought that, the gardener, Henry Beaumont, did it.'

'Yes. He disappeared the day that Rachael Carmichael fell from the cliff. I put in train a search for him, of course, but not long after, I left the case. I'm afraid I can't comment on what happened after that. Why he was never found or why the case was abandoned, I have no idea.'

'I know you left the case early, Reg, but what were your thoughts concerning Rachael when you began the investigation? For example, did you think she was alone when she went over that cliff?'

'You mean do I think it was an accident or suicide?' Fellowes rubbed his chin. 'Mmm. Good question. I seem to remember that when I first arrived at the scene, there was evidence to suggest - only suggest, mind - that the victim was not alone.'

'What kind of evidence?' asked Fitzjohn.

'We found a half smoked cigarette on the grass next to her easel. Recently smoked, and it wasn't hers. Rachael didn't smoke. It was thought it may have been dropped by the gardener who, according to the housekeeper, was a smoker.' Fellowes paused. 'Other than the housekeeper and the two children, the only other person at Lane's End that day was Rachael's brother-in-law, Sebastian Newberry. He didn't smoke either. He arrived at Lane's End mid-afternoon and raised the alarm. Richard Carmichael arrived at about five-thirty. He'd been working in the city. We checked that out. It was confirmed. He'd been in a meeting since early morning. Of course, when we went to question Henry Beaumont, we found he'd packed his things and left. And as far as Rachael is concerned, her body was found washed up on North Palm Beach forty-eight hours later. That's all I can tell you, I'm afraid. I'm sorry, Alistair.'

Fitzjohn arrived home that evening to find Meg's suitcase in the front hall. 'Meg?' he called as he placed the mail on the hall table and put his briefcase down.

'Home at last, I see,' came the sound of Meg's voice. Fitzjohn turned to see his sister descending the staircase.

'I know it's late, Meg, but we can still discuss Sophie's situation if you wish.' Fitzjohn looked down at the suitcase. 'There's no reason to go home in a huff.'

'I'm not going home, Alistair. And I'm not in a huff. I've been invited to stay with Sophie for a few days.' Fitzjohn gaped at his sister. 'You needn't look so surprised.'

'I'm not. I'm... I'm just glad that you and Sophie have come to an agreement about her living arrangements.'

'Ah, well. That's still to be determined. I'll do that after my visit.'

'How do Sophie's room-mates feel about your staying with them?'

'Brian and Andrew? They're pleased, of course. It was their idea that I stay for a few days.'

'It was?' Fitzjohn's brow furrowed. 'You mean Sophie doesn't know?'

'Not when I was invited. She wasn't at the apartment when I visited, but I'm sure she knows by now.' Meg gave a quick smile before she glanced at her reflection in the hall mirror. 'You didn't tell me her roommates are gay, Alistair.'

'I didn't know.' Fitzjohn paused. 'I hope that doesn't colour your judgment, Meg.'

'Not in the least. If anything, I think it's a definite plus.' Meg zipped up her handbag and hooked it on her shoulder. 'We don't have to worry about hanky panky, do we?' she continued, looking at her watch. 'They should be here shortly. Now Alistair, I've left some dinner for you in the oven and I've cleaned out the fridge. I threw out a lot of things that are just not healthy eating.' Meg paused. 'Now, I think I have everything but I'm sure there was something else I had to tell you. What was it now? Ah, yes. It's about that next door neighbour of yours.'

'Which one? Not Rhonda Butler?'

'If that's the one whose tree fell on your greenhouse last autumn, then, yes. She dropped by earlier this evening to tell you... actually her words were "to warn you", that she's going to complain to the council about your new greenhouse. Apparently the roof, being so much higher than the old greenhouse roof, is reflecting the afternoon sun through her kitchen window and blinding her while she's doing the dishes. She's going to demand that you have the greenhouse removed.'

'*She's what?*'

'Don't shout at me, Alistair. I'm merely the messenger. Although I did tell her that she has Buckley's chance and that if I lived here she wouldn't get past the front gate.'

Fitzjohn gaped at his sister. 'You said that to Rhonda Butler?'

'Yes. Perhaps I shouldn't have but I was quite incensed at the time' As Meg spoke the doorbell rang. 'Ah. That'll be Brian and Andrew. Got to run.' She gave a quick smile.

Still reeling from Meg's reproach to Rhonda, Fitzjohn opened the door. As he did so three faces appeared, one of them Sophie's. Meg bustled off with the two young men in tow, while Sophie turned to her uncle.

'I'm sorry about this,' Fitzjohn said.

'It's not your fault, Uncle Alistair. We'll manage, somehow. Brian and Andrew were taken by surprise. I wasn't at home when Mum called around, you see. They didn't realise what was happening until Mum had invited herself.'

'Then all I can say is good luck.'

Fitzjohn leaned against the door as it shut and he sighed. 'Rhonda, the bane of my existence.' Pushing himself off the door, he walked slowly through the house to the kitchen, poured himself a glass of whisky, and made his way out into the back garden. With the birds roosting in the trees and no hint of a breeze, the evening lay peaceful and quiet. He sat down in one of the garden chairs, and took a sip of his whisky before his eyes came to rest on the greenhouse, now a silhouette against the evening sky. *If you think I'm tearing that down, Rhonda Butler, you've got another think coming.*

☞ CHAPTER 14 ☜

Fitzjohn arrived in his office at dawn the following morning and settled himself at his desk. In the early hour before the hubbub began, his thoughts traversed the Peter Van Goren case until a knock sounded and Betts came into the room. Fitzjohn set his pen down, somewhat disappointed at the interruption. 'Morning, Betts.'

'Morning, sir. I thought I'd get in early because we're speaking to Amanda Marsh first thing, aren't we?'

'I am, but I want you to make a concerted effort to find out more about Peter Van Goren. There has to be something we've missed concerning his link to the Carmichael family. Without it, our investigation doesn't make sense. I'll take Williams with me.'

With Williams at the wheel and displaying a certain amount of preoccupation, the two officers made their way in silence to Glebe and the home of Amanda Marsh. Fitzjohn's thoughts dwelled for a time on Rhonda Butler's threat. No doubt he could expect a letter from the Council in a matter of days if last year's debacle over her tree was anything to go by.

'This is it, sir,' said Williams, breaking the silence.

Brought back from his thoughts, Fitzjohn peered out of the passenger window at a two-storey Victorian terrace house, its upper balcony trimmed with rich iron lacework. Climbing out of the car, he led the way through the small garden to the front door and rang the bell, all too aware of Williams's reticence. When the door opened, Amanda appeared. In the light of day she looked older than she had the night Peter Van Goren had died. Even so, she was impeccably dressed in a pair of light green slacks and a white blouse, her bright blue eyes contrasting her short silver grey hair.

'Good morning, Ms Marsh,' said Fitzjohn with a smile.

'Morning,' she replied with a look of surprise.

'We have a few more questions we'd like to ask,' Fitzjohn continued. 'Can we come in?'

'I was about to leave for the office,' Amanda replied, looking at her watch. 'Will it take long?'

'I shouldn't think so.'

'Very well.' Amanda led the way into a small sitting room, its furnishing matching the era of the house. 'Is there news about the man who died at the Observatory?' she asked, sitting down while Fitzjohn and Williams settled themselves on the sofa.

'Not yet, but events have necessitated that we speak to you again.'

'Well, I'm sure I told you everything I know when we were at the Observatory the other night, Chief Inspector.'

'It's not about the death of Peter Van Goren, Ms Marsh. In the course of our investigation, it's come to light that you once worked for the Carmichael's as a housekeeper.'

'Yes. Didn't I mention that before? I started working for them shortly after their first child was born. That would have been in 1978, if I remember correctly.'

'And when did you leave their employ?'

'Let's see. That would have been in 1983. Not long after Mrs Carmichael died.' Amanda paused. 'The first Mrs Carmichael, that is. Do you know about that?'

'Yes. Rachael Carmichael. We understand she died at Whale Beach.'

'That's right.' Amanda quivered. 'Her death still haunts me.'

'Can you tell us what you remember about that day, Ms Marsh?'

'I can. As if it was yesterday, Chief Inspector. It's replayed in my mind many times. It was a Friday. I'd accompanied Mrs Carmichael and the two children to Lane's End, at Whale Beach. It was a property the family owned so that they could get away from the city from time to time. We were to spend the long weekend there. Mr Carmichael was to join us that evening. The gardener met us when we arrived and helped us in with the bags and soon after, Mrs Carmichael went off to paint as she always did. She was an artist, you see. She used a small cottage on the property as her studio.' Amanda thought for a moment. 'I spent the morning looking after the children and getting the house organised for our stay before I prepared lunch.'

'Did Mrs Carmichael return to the house for lunch?'

'No. I took a salad down to the cottage for her at mid-day.'

'And where were the children while you did that?' asked Fitzjohn.

'Oh. Let me see. Ben was out following the gardener around as he always did, and I took Joanna, the baby, with me.'

'Was Rachael in the cottage when you arrived?'

'No. It was such a beautiful day, she said she'd decided to sit outside. She'd set her easel up on the grass outside the cottage.'

'And how did she seem at the time?'

'Very content. She loved being at Lane's End.' Amanda paused in reflection.

'Did you see her again that day?'

'No. I never saw her again.' Amanda Marsh's voice broke and she grabbed a tissue from the coffee table to stem her tears. 'You'll have to excuse me. Talking about it brings it all back.'

Fitzjohn waited before he continued. 'Are you all right to go on, Ms Marsh?' Amanda nodded. 'Can you tell us what happened after you left Mrs Carmichael that day?'

'I returned to the house and had lunch with the children. After that, Ben went back out to play and I put Joanna down for her afternoon nap. Not long after, Mr Newberry arrived. He's Richard Carmichael's half-brother. Or at least he was. I asked him if he'd like to sit down and have some lunch, but he said he wanted to go and speak to Rachael first. It wasn't long though before he was back saying he couldn't find her. That's when the day became a nightmare. Lane's End is such a big place. I told him she might have wandered off to paint on the other side of the cove so he went back out but, of course, he didn't find her. When he arrived back the second time, he called the police and also his brother, Richard.'

'Where was the gardener while all this was going on?' asked Fitzjohn.

'Henry? Well, at the time, I assumed he was helping Mr Newberry look for Mrs Carmichael, but I later learnt that he'd packed his belongings and left. Of course, it raised suspicion that he had something to do with Rachael's death, although I've always found that hard to believe. What reason could he have to hurt Mrs Carmichael, but there again, why else would he disappear at a time like that?' Amanda threw her hands in the air.

'What sort of a person was Henry Beaumont, Ms Marsh?'

'Well, as I remember, he was a fairly quiet man. Kept to himself a lot, but he was a good worker. He transformed the grounds at Lane's End into a botanical masterpiece.'

With thoughts tumbling through his mind including Williams's continued silence, the two officers returned to the station and went their separate ways. Fitzjohn got himself a cup of coffee and went to his office to prepare for the next case management meeting. It wasn't long, however, before Williams appeared in the open doorway.

'Can I speak to you, sir?' he asked.

'Can't it wait for the meeting, Williams? I just want to get a few things straight in my mind before we start.'

'It's not about the case, sir,' replied Williams, looking un-characteristically awkward.

'Oh?'

'No. It's... more or less personal.'

Fitzjohn put his pen down and sat back in his chair. 'Then you'd better come in and close the door.' He gestured to the chairs in front of his desk.

Williams sat down and rubbed the back of his neck. 'I'm not sure how to start, sir.'

'Why don't you start with what it's about?'

'Okay. It's about someone on staff.' Williams hesitated. 'Someone of higher rank.'

'Me?' asked Fitzjohn.

'No, not you, sir. It's about Chief Superintendent Grieg.'

'Oh.' Fitzjohn sat forward. 'What about him?'

'Do you remember during your secondment to Kings Cross Station last autumn when you found I'd been permanently moved there by the Chief?'

'Yes.'

'Well, as I think I told you at the time, I was happy with the move until...'

Fitzjohn frowned. 'Until what?'

'This will sound ridiculous...God, I can hardly believe I'm sitting here telling you.'

'You haven't told me anything yet, Williams.'

'Well, it's just that I have the feeling my transfer to Kings Cross was set up for a purpose not related to my career in the police force.' Williams's eyes locked onto Fitzjohn's. 'I'm probably not making myself very clear here, am I?' Williams ran his trembling hand through his hair. 'You see, sir, I'd been at Kings Cross Station for about a week when you arrived. After your arrival, Chief Superintendent Grieg contacted me and told me to report to him on the case you were working on at the time.'

'The Michael Rossi case?'

'Yes. Chief Superintendent Grieg said he wanted to know everything that went on.' Williams paused. 'It went against the grain, but I'm afraid I did what he told me to do.'

'So why are you telling me this now?' asked Fitzjohn.

'Because... Oh, God.' Williams took a deep breath. 'Because last week, I found myself transferred back here to Day Street and this morning before we left to interview Amanda Marsh, the Chief Superintendent told me to do the same again. I'm to report to him on your activities in relation to the Van Goren case. There, I've said it.' Williams slumped back in his chair.

'Did the Chief Superintendent give you a reason?' asked Fitzjohn.

'No, sir, but he did make it clear that it wouldn't be in my best interest to refuse. I got the feeling I'd end up transferred to the farthest reaches of New South Wales. What should I do, sir?'

'Well, first let me say that I appreciate your coming to see me because I know how difficult it must have been for you, especially since it concerns a senior officer. Secondly, I apologise for the manner in which you've been treated. And as far as what you should do, I'd say there's nothing you need to do. I'll see to this matter myself and we'll speak again when I've done so.'

As Williams left the office, Fitzjohn sat back in his chair. So, he thought, Williams was and, it seems, still is Grieg's mole. What possible motive could Grieg have for enlisting a junior officer to spy? Is he paranoid enough to think I want his job? If so, what lengths will he go to get rid of me? As these thoughts ran through his head, Betts appeared.

'The Duty Sergeant said you want to see me, sir,' he said, striding into the room.

'Yes, Betts. I want to know if there's any news on Van Goren before we go into the case management meeting.'

'There is, sir. We've ascertained that Peter Van Goren's bank account records started in October, 1983. He had no records prior to that. In Australia, at least. I've contacted Interpol. I'm just waiting to hear back.'

'Good. So, we could conclude that before then he lived overseas. With a name like Van Goren, he might have been an immigrant. Didn't Ida Clegg mention that he spoke with a slight accent?'

'She did,' replied Betts, standing with both hands on the back of one of the chairs in front of Fitzjohn's desk. 'But when I checked with the Immigration Department, I found there is no record of anybody by the name of Peter Van Goren entering Australia as either an immigrant or a tourist, which only leaves the possibility that he came into the country illegally.'

'But how?' mused Fitzjohn.

'Well, there are a few possibilities. He could have entered as a tourist and changed his name when he overstayed his visa. Or he might have come in as an employee of some foreign company and never left. Then there's the possibility he worked for a shipping line and jumped ship.'

'Check them all, Betts.' Fitzjohn thought for a moment. 'It's not that easy to open a bank account. What did he use as verification?'

'His Australian passport, sir.'

'Really? How did he manage that one, I wonder.'

'Not through the usual channels,' replied Betts. 'I contacted the Passport Office in Canberra. They have no record of issuing a passport in the name Peter Van Goren.'

'A forgery then. Not difficult to get, I suppose, if you know the right people.' Fitzjohn looked thoughtful.

'There's something else, sir. His bank records show that his initial account in 1983, was opened with a sizeable amount. Twenty-five thousand dollars. Quite a sum at the time, I imagine.'

'It was, Betts. Enough to get him started with his first business venture, I'd say.'

'I think it did, sir, because on checking with Raymond West, Van Goren opened his first coffee shop around that time. West did the conveyancing.'

'Very well. Why don't we make ourselves familiar with Mr Van Goren's business ventures because we don't seem to be making much headway in any other area? To start with, arrange for a search warrant to search his home at Vaucluse. Hopefully it'll help us get a better perspective on the man.' Fitzjohn paused. 'The other thing I want to discuss is Rachael Carmichael. I know her death isn't part of our investigation, but with that case left unsolved and the fact that our present case involves the same family, I feel we should keep it in mind. If nothing else, it could give us some insight into those who are of interest to us in the Peter Van Goren case.'

Fitzjohn flicked through the papers on his desk. 'For a start, Amanda Marsh's recollections about the day Rachael died, match that of Sebastian Newberry. Secondly, if there was a problem between Amanda and Rachael, there's been no hint of it from those we've spoken to. Even Newberry's relationship with Rachael appears to have been that of true friendship. Henry Beaumont, of course, remains an enigma. All we know about him is that he was, presumably, a good gardener. According to Amanda Marsh, that is.

'Well, if Rachael's death was foul play, sir, there were only three people who saw her alone that day. Amanda, Newberry and Henry Beaumont, and it seems to me that they each had the opportunity and the means to kill her. Beaumont, in particular. He had ample time to be alone with her that morning while she was painting at the cottage, and let's not forget, he disappeared after she was found to be missing.'

'But why, Betts? What motive would he have to kill her? Come to that, what motive would any of them have had?'

'Maybe we're reading too much into it, sir. Maybe she did jump or accidentally slip.'

'It still doesn't explain why Henry packed up and left that day. Unless, of course, it was foul play and he knew the per-petrator. If that was the case, whoever that person was must have had something on Henry Beaumont to cause him to leave. See what you can find out about him, Betts.'

'Excuse me, Chief Inspector.' Fitzjohn and Betts looked around to see the Duty Officer standing in the doorway. 'There's a Mr Ben Carmichael here to see you.'

Fitzjohn glanced at Betts who went to stand next to the filing cabinet. 'Thank you, Sergeant. You can show him in.'

'He must be here about his fiancée,' said Betts.'

'Mmm. I dare say he is. There's been no new development on that as yet, has there?'

'No, sir. I spoke to DCI Roberts only this morning.'

'Then we'll have to disappoint him, I'm afraid.'

'Mr Carmichael,' said Fitzjohn as Ben appeared in the doorway. 'Please, come in and have a seat. I'm afraid there's no news as yet on your fiancée's attacker.'

'Actually, I'm not here about that, Chief Inspector. I wanted to speak to you about another matter. It's concerning Peter Van Goren.' Ben Carmichael settled himself into a chair. 'To come straight to the point, I've just learnt that he made me a beneficiary in his will.' Ben looked at Fitzjohn. 'You probably think that I've been lying to you all along about our relationship, but I haven't. I didn't know the man.'

'Even so, you have to agree that it's unusual for someone to leave their estate to a total stranger,' replied Fitzjohn.'

'I agree, and I can't think why he did it.' Ben paused. 'I'd hate you to think that my father was involved in some way.'

'We can't discount it.'

'That's what I was afraid of.' Ben shook his head. 'You didn't know my father, Chief Inspector. He was a decent, hard-working man. He didn't kill Peter Van Goren.'

'We're not saying he did, but we are of the opinion that your father knew him. How, we don't know, but we will find out. If you know anything, anything at all, I do urge you to come forward with that information.' Fitzjohn paused for a moment before he continued. 'We understand you were quite young when your mother died, Mr Carmichael.'

Ben hesitated as if taken aback by the sudden change in subject. 'Yes. I was six at the time.'

'Do you remember what happened on that day?'

'Up until the day I found Emma at Lane's End, I didn't remember much about it at all.'

'And since?' asked Fitzjohn.

'Since then I've remembered a few things.'

'Like what?'

'Like the fact that we had a gardener. I now remember him meeting us and helping with the bags when we arrived. It sounds ridiculous but I'd forgotten all about him.'

'It's not surprising,' said Fitzjohn. 'After all, it must have been a confusing and traumatic day for you. Can you tell us anything about the man?'

Ben smiled as if to himself. 'Only that he had a lot of time for me. He let me follow him around while he worked.' Ben's brow wrinkled. 'I also remember asking him where he was going the day he left.' Ben paused. 'There were tears in his eyes.'

'You saw him leave?' asked Fitzjohn.

'Yes.'

'Did you tell anyone?'

'I don't know. All I remember is being driven back home to Mosman and wondering why we weren't staying for the weekend like we'd planned. And wondering why my mother wasn't with us. My questions remained unanswered. The rest is a blank.'

Fitzjohn studied Ben Carmichael's face before he continued. 'If you do think of anything else about that day, Mr Carmichael, will you come and see us?'

'Yes, of course.' Ben met Fitzjohn's intent gaze. 'Why is that day so important, Chief Inspector?'

'It may not be, Mr Carmichael, but we can't dismiss anything at this point in our investigation.'

'Then perhaps I should tell you that Lane's End has been left to me in my father's will.'

'I see. Well, in light of that fact, can I ask whether selling the property is part of your plan? Because if it is, we'd ask that you delay putting it on the market until our investigation is complete.'

'I have no plans. Not at this stage.' Ben Carmichael met Fitzjohn's. 'Does this mean that you think Lane's End has something to do with Peter Van Goren's death?'

'As I mentioned earlier,' replied Fitzjohn. 'We can't discount anything.'

☞ CHAPTER 15 ☜

Under a blanket of low dark cloud and with dawn breaking, the taxi wended its way through the streets of Sydney's CBD. Fitzjohn gazed out of the rain splattered window, his thoughts a mixture of Rhonda Butler's threat of Council action against his beloved greenhouse, and the mystery surrounding Peter Van Goren's true identity. When the taxi pulled up in front of Day Street Police Station, he climbed out, and holding his morning paper above his head, raced inside. Amid the hubbub, he made his way to his office where he placed his wet briefcase down before tossing the sodden newspaper onto the desk. As he did so, the door opened and Betts walked into the room, a certain sense of satisfaction across his face.

'Morning, Betts,' said Fitzjohn, turning around. 'You look particularly cheery for such a wet morning. Why's that?'

'I have news about Peter Van Goren, sir.'

'Oh?' Fitzjohn grabbed the paper and tried to extract the crossword section. 'What sort of news?'

'Ida Clegg contacted me last night after you'd left, and before our search warrant had come through from the Magistrate's office. She said she'd been going through Mr Van Goren's belongings and had come across a couple of items she thought we should see. One of them was a merchant seaman's card in the name of Henry Beaumont.' The newspaper fell from Fitzjohn's hands. 'And that's not all, sir. Mrs Clegg also found an envelope containing x-rays, taken at Mona Vale Hospital in 1982. Of a leg! They're in the name of Henry Beaumont.'

'So, what you're saying is that Van Goren and Henry Beaumont are one and the same person.' Fitzjohn sat down heavily into his chair.

'Yes,' replied Betts. 'I checked with the hospital archive records. They confirmed that at the time of admission, Mr Beaumont was employed as a gardener at Lane's End. It's all there, sir. How he injured his leg while using a lawn mower on a hillside at his place of employment, Lane's End, as well as his medical expenses being paid by his employer, Richard Carmichael.'

'That's all well and good, Betts, but we'll need more proof than the fact that these x-rays were found at Van Goren's residence.'

'We have that too, sir. Comparing the records of Henry Beaumont to those of Peter Van Goren at the morgue - blood group, everything. It all matches!' Betts smiled.

'Well done. I'm impressed. Finally, we have a positive connection between Van Goren and the Carmichael family.' Fitzjohn swung his chair back and forth. 'Who would have thought? Van Goren, alias Henry Beaumont, knew Richard

Carmichael because he'd worked as the family's gardener. But what was his reason for attending the cocktail party, I wonder? That's the next question.'

'Now we know who Van Goren really was, I'd say it was something to do with Rachael's death,' replied Betts. 'After all, if we go back thirty years to September 1983, we know that Henry disappeared without trace the day she fell from the cliff. That gave rise to the suspicion that he might have been involved in her death. Fast forward to March 2013, Henry, now known as Peter Van Goren, attends the cocktail party at the Observatory after being told, that afternoon, he had a matter of weeks to live. Maybe the fact he'd absconded that day prompted him to seek out Richard Carmichael to either admit or deny his involvement. Not to mention the fact that if he wasn't responsible, he might have known who was.'

'So, we can surmise that if he was there to tell Richard Carmichael that he was responsible, that admission alone would have given Richard Carmichael a motive to kill Van Goren,' said Fitzjohn. 'On the other hand, if Van Goren was there to deny perpetrating such a heinous act, it might have been the catalyst for Carmichael's collapse, and subsequent heart attack. The confusion that followed his collapse would have allowed the killer ample time to ensure Van Goren couldn't tell anyone else. But if that was the case, Betts, who was it?'

'I think Sebastian Newberry and Amanda Marsh are the most likely suspects, sir. They were the only two people at the function who were also at Lane's End when Rachael died.'

'True, if we're connecting Rachael's death with Van Goren's.' Fitzjohn thought for a moment. 'Could there have been someone else at Lane's End the day Rachael died that we don't know about?'

'If there was, surely the housekeeper or Newberry would have known.'

'Not necessarily. Remember, Lane's End is a big place. There might be another way of getting to Ivy Cottage without passing by the main house.'

'I'll see what I can find out, sir.'

'Do that, because now we know Peter Van Goren's true identity, it begs belief that none of the guests at that cocktail party who had known Henry Beaumont, didn't recognise him. He couldn't have changed that much over the years. Even if he had, surely the sight of that silver handled cane would have jogged their memories.' Fitzjohn sat back in his chair. 'One thing's for sure. We're not getting the whole truth from one, or perhaps more than one of those we interviewed. We'll question them all again, but this time formally. Make the arrangements, starting with Mr Newberry.'

'Yes, sir.'

The police officer opened the door into Interview Room #2 and stood back. 'If you'll take a seat in there, gentlemen, DCI Fitzjohn will be with you shortly.'

Scowling, Sebastian, followed by his solicitor, strode into the small windowless room and looked around. 'God, it reminds me of one of those police shows I watch on television... except this is for real.' With indignation, he yanked out a chair from the table and plumped down, his gaze taking in the insipid green walls. 'What on earth am I doing here? I should have insisted they speak to me at home or at my office.' As the minutes ticked by, he tapped the leg of the table with the point of his shoe. 'How long are we going to have to wait? I've got better things to do with my time.'

'It shouldn't be too long now,' replied the solicitor in a low voice. 'And remember, Sebastian, you're not obliged to answer any questions.' As he spoke, the door opened and Fitzjohn walked into the room, followed by Betts.

'Sorry to keep you, Mr Newberry,' said Fitzjohn as he sat down and placed his papers on the table. He glanced at Betts who prepared the recording device and once introductions had been made, started the interview. 'Now, firstly...'

'Why have I been made to come here, Chief Inspector?' interrupted Newberry. 'Especially since I've told you everything I know about that man's death at the Observatory.'

'We don't want to ask you about Peter Van Goren, Mr Newberry. We'd like to talk to you about your brother, Richard, and his family.'

Newberry tugged at his ear. 'What on earth for? How can that help? My brother's dead.'

Unmoved by Newberry's outburst, Fitzjohn clasped his hands together and replied, 'Because it will enable us to build a picture. A sort of background, if you like, on the Carmichael family and how others in our present investigation, like yourself, are connected to them. It helps give us a better perspective. I'm sure you find that yourself when dealing with your clients. You need to know their likes and dislikes, whereas I like to know where people come from and how they're linked.' Fitzjohn gave a quick smile. Sebastian

Newberry opened his mouth to speak, but Fitzjohn ignored the gesture and continued. 'So, let's begin again. Shall we?' Sebastian slumped back in his chair. 'When last we spoke, you said you and your half-brother, Richard, were close.'

'Yes. We were,' Newberry replied. 'I still can't believe he's gone. His passing has changed all our lives. Mine, his children's and his wife, Laura's. What she must be going through, I can't imagine.' He glared at Fitzjohn. 'Have you any idea what it's like to lose someone close to you, Chief Inspector?'

Fitzjohn ignored the question. 'We understand that Laura Carmichael is your half-brother's second wife,' continued Fitzjohn.

'Yes. She is. Richard was first married to Rachael. She died in tragic circumstances. Richard never got over it.' Newberry paused. 'I introduced them, you know.'

'Oh? How did you and Rachael come to know each other, Mr Newberry?'

'We met while we were at art school in the days when I still believed in my artistic talents.' Newberry chuckled to himself. 'Eventually, I came to my senses and became an architect. Rachael carried on, of course, and became relatively successful. I did a bit of marketing and distribution of her work from time to time.' Newberry frowned. 'Forgive me, Chief Inspector, but where is this leading?'

'We'd like your thoughts on what happened at Lane's End the day that Rachael died,' replied Fitzjohn.

'Why? I can't see how it will help you with your present investigation.'

'Nevertheless, we'd appreciate your recollection.'

'All right, if I must, but I still don't see the point. After all, it happened thirty odd years ago.' Newberry sighed, displaying his annoyance. 'Let's see. If I remember correctly, it was a long weekend and I was to spend it at Lane's End with Richard and Rachael. I arrived about one-thirty on the Friday afternoon. Amanda Marsh, she was the housekeeper at the time, greeted me. You met Amanda, of course, at the cocktail party.' Fitzjohn nodded. 'She told me Rachael was down at Ivy Cottage painting so I set off but when I got there, she wasn't at the cottage or anywhere roundabout although her easel was set out on the grass, as if she'd just stepped away from it for a moment. I wondered whether she might have gone back to the house, perhaps by another route so I decided to walk back. When I got there, of course, she wasn't there. Amanda suggested she might have gone for a walk to the other side of the cove so I went out again, but there was no sign of her. As you can imagine, by this time, I was frantic. I retraced my steps back towards the cottage although I did make a small detour at one stage, along the edge of the cliff but I found nothing to suggest she'd fallen over. Later, of course, I realised that her body had already been washed off the rocks.' Sebastian reflected for a moment. 'I hate to think about that day. Let alone talk about it.'

'Unfortunately, it's necessary that we ask these questions, I'm afraid,' replied Fitzjohn, studying Newberry's face, whose eyes were cast down. 'What happened next?'

'I returned to the house and called the police, and Richard, of course. God! It was the hardest phone call I've ever had to make.' Sebastian shook his head.

'Tell us about the gardener your brother employed. Henry Beaumont, was it?'

Sebastian crossed his arms and eyed Fitzjohn. 'Yes, it was. What about him?'

'Where was Henry while the search for Rachael was going on?'

'I have no idea. I didn't see him until I was on my way back to the house to make the calls. I told him that Rachael was missing and I was going to contact the police. That's the last I saw of the man. Obviously, after we spoke, he packed his bags and left. The police never found him. But I suppose you know that.'

'We do,' replied Fitzjohn. 'Makes one think that Henry had something to do with Rachael's death, doesn't it? After all, why else would he leave so suddenly? What are your thoughts, Mr Newberry? 'Do you think Rachael slipped, jumped, or do you think there was foul play involved?'

'I've thought about it a lot over the years and I can tell you this. Rachael wouldn't have committed suicide. She had no reason to. After all, she was happily married to my brother and enthusiastic about her work. She could have slipped, of course, but I doubt it. She never ventured too close to the cliff edge.'

'So, what are you saying, that there *was* foul play involved in her death?'

'Yes. I am.'

'In that case, who do you think did it, keeping in mind that there was only yourself, Henry Beaumont and Amanda Marsh at Lane's End that afternoon? Unless, of course, someone else had arrived to see Rachael and used another entrance to get to Ivy Cottage.'

'That wouldn't have been possible. At that time, the land around Lane's End was undeveloped and inaccessible,' replied Newberry.

'In that case, we're left with the three of you, aren't we?' said Fitzjohn with a bemused smile.

'Well, it certainly wasn't me, but it could have been either of the other two.'

'Why do you say that?' Fitzjohn clasped his hands together underneath his chin.

'Because, as I said before, Henry disappeared that day, right after I told him I was calling the police. Why would he do that? He must have had some reason for not wanting to be there when the police arrived.'

'And what about Amanda Marsh?' asked Fitzjohn. 'Why do you think she could have killed Rachael?'

Sebastian gave a chuckle. 'Because she was in love with Richard, of course. Why do you think she reinvented herself as a caterer and wormed her way back into his life after Rachael's death, for heaven's sake?'

Fitzjohn's brow wrinkled. 'Was your brother aware of what you're suggesting?'

'If he was, he never spoke about it to me. Richard wasn't interested in Amanda in that way. As far as he was concerned, she was a loyal employee while she was his housekeeper and a good caterer later on.' Newberry looked at his watch. 'Is this going to take much longer because I've got clients to see?'

'Not too much longer,' replied Fitzjohn with a slight smile. 'I just want to touch on Peter Van Goren before we terminate the interview. 'You see, we've discovered that Mr Van Goren was actually the man you knew as Henry Beaumont.' Sebastian stared at Fitzjohn for a long moment without replying. 'Surely if you didn't recognise him on the night he appeared at the cocktail party, the silver cane that he carried would have jiggled your memory. After all, Henry walked with just such a cane, didn't he?' Fitzjohn waited for Newberry to reply. 'Well?'

A sheen of sweat appeared across Sebastian's forehead. 'All right. I knew it was him.'

'Then why did you tell us you didn't know Peter Van Goren?'

'Because... I thought if it was discovered who Van Goren really was, it would restart the investigation into Rachael's death, and I knew that Richard wouldn't survive going through all that again.' Newberry sighed. 'As it turned out, he didn't.'

'The Hunts and Amanda Marsh also denied knowing Peter Van Goren. Was that your doing?' asked Fitzjohn.

'It might have been my idea, but I didn't have to twist their arms. None of them wanted to revisit the circumstances surrounding Rachael's death.'

'What about the argument you and your brother had after he'd spoken to Van Goren? It wasn't about a business matter, was it? Mr Van Goren told Richard that it was you who had pushed Rachael off that cliff? Is that what enraged Richard, Mr Newberry?'

'*For heaven's sake!*' Sebastian Newberry's chair fell backwards as he stood up, his face red with rage. 'You've got your nerve accusing *me* of murder! How *dare* you?'

Unperturbed by the outburst, Fitzjohn sat back, his eyes locked onto Newberry's. 'Where were you on Saturday, March 26th?' he asked.

'*What?*'

'Were you at Lane's End, Mr Newberry?'

'Lane's End? Why would I be there?' Newberry picked up his chair and sat down again. 'If you must know, I was out doing quotes for jobs. I do so every Saturday.'

'Then perhaps you can give DS Betts the names and addresses of the people you saw, as well as the times that you saw them.'

'Do you believe Newberry's reason for not wanting to recognise Peter Van Goren, sir?' asked Betts as he and Fitzjohn left the interview room.

'It sounds plausible enough and I tend to believe him because his admission does give him a motive to kill Van Goren. He's a fairly astute man, so I'm sure he's aware of that fact. And there's something else, Betts. We can now assume that Peter Van Goren's death is connected to Rachael's, and I can't see that Newberry had a motive to kill her.'

'What about Amanda Marsh? What he told us about her being in love with Richard Carmichael does give her a motive.'

'You're right. It does. Let's see what else we can glean from that fact when we interview her again. But first, I want you to check out Newberry's alibi concerning Saturday, March 26th. The day that Emma Phillips was attacked at Lane's End. While you're doing that, I'll speak to Laura Carmichael. In light of what Newberry has just told us and since she's Richard's second wife, I'd like to know what she thinks about Amanda Marsh.'

Later that morning and accompanied by Williams, Fitzjohn arrived at the Carmichael home in Mosman. He winced as he peered out of the passenger window at the steps leading up through the front garden to the house. Williams followed his gaze. 'We can look on this as our exercise for the day, sir.'

'I don't need that much exercise, Williams,' replied Fitzjohn as he started the climb. When they neared the top, they found a woman in her early fifties pruning a row of standard white roses, her short, auburn hair hiding underneath a golf cap.

'Mrs Carmichael?' asked Fitzjohn, by now out of breath.

Laura turned, her hazel eyes looking guardedly at the two officers. 'Yes. Can I help you?'

Fitzjohn held up his warrant card and introduced himself.

Laura's face brightened. 'Ah. We meet at last, Chief Inspector,' she replied, placing her secateurs in the basket at her feet before removing her gardening gloves. 'My step-daughter, Joanna, told me she'd spoken to you about that dreadful night at the Observatory. I'm not sure I can add much to what she told you, but do come inside.' Laura removed her cap, placed it on the hall table and led the way through to the sunroom where Fitzjohn and Betts had spoken earlier to Joanna. 'Have you found out who the man who died was?' she asked.

'Yes, we have,' replied Fitzjohn as they sat down. 'He was a business man, but Peter Van Goren wasn't his name. His real name was Henry Beaumont.'

'Beaumont? That's odd.' Laura frowned.

'Have you heard the name before, Mrs Carmichael? In connection with your family, that is?'

'Yes, I have, as a matter of fact. I came across it the other day when I was going through papers in my husband's study. Apparently, a Mr Beaumont used to work for Richard years ago as a gardener at Lane's End. Lane's End is a property he owned at Whale Beach. Henry Beaumont must have been injured while at work because Richard paid his medical expenses. That was what the papers were about. All to do with the medical bills.' Laura looked at Fitzjohn. 'This must mean that my husband knew the man who died at the cocktail party, doesn't it?'

'It seems so,' replied Fitzjohn.

'I can't understand it. Richard gave no indication he knew the man.'

'We understand Emerson Hunt contacted your husband late on Friday night.'

'Yes, he did ring to tell Richard about what had happened there after we'd left.' Laura paused. 'It was after that phone call that my husband suffered his heart attack.' A long silence followed before Laura Carmichael continued. 'Do you know why Mr Van Goren came to the cocktail party, Chief Inspector?'

'No,' said Fitzjohn.

'It's strange that he'd changed his name from Beaumont. I wonder why?'

'That much we do know, but, at this stage, we're not at liberty to say. Tell me, Mrs Carmichael, did your husband ever speak to you about his first wife, Rachael?'

Laura gave Fitzjohn a quizzical look. 'Yes, he did speak of her, but only when he and I first met. After that, it was a closed subject. I think the way in which she died haunted Richard.' Laura Carmichael caught Fitzjohn's gaze. 'Why do you ask? Are you aware of the circumstances of her death?' Fitzjohn nodded. 'Mmm. I thought you might be. You probably know more than me. The little I gleaned from our talks, I passed on to Ben and Joanna when they started to ask questions about their mother. But I'm sure there's much I don't know.'

'Did your husband say what he thought happened to Rachael?'

'Not in so many words. Because the reason for her death could never be proved, I believe he liked to think it was an accident. That she'd slipped on the path. You see, for him, her death was like an open door that could never be closed.' Laura Carmichael paused. 'I've lived with her ghost for almost thirty years, Chief Inspector.'

'Can we ask you about the woman who found Mr Van Goren's body?'

'It was the caterer, wasn't it, Amanda Marsh?'

'Yes. We understand that Ms Marsh worked for your husband as a housekeeper at one time.'

'Yes, she did. I think that's why Richard always used her catering business for the company's functions. He said she'd been a good employee. To be honest, I think he felt guilty about having to let her go after Rachael died. Apparently, his mother moved in here to look after the children and Richard so Amanda's services were no longer needed. That was before we met, of course.'

'I see. Tell me, Mrs Carmichael, how do you get on with Amanda Marsh?'

'Fine. She appears to be very efficient at what she does. Of course, I have very little to do with her. Catering for functions held by Carmichael Hunt Real Estate is managed through Richard's office. I just attend the functions. Or at least I did.'

'But you did see Amanda at times.'

'Yes, but only if she was understaffed and came along to help. As she did the night Mr Van Goren died.' When Fitzjohn did not reply, Laura continued. 'Oh, I see. You want to know what I think about Amanda Marsh on a personal level.' Laura ran her hand along the arm of her chair, following its pattern with her index finger. 'Well, to be quite honest, I don't like the woman. I never have.'

'Can you tell us why?'

'I prefer not to if you don't mind,' replied Laura. 'I don't necessarily like to voice my opinion about someone I don't particularly like.'

'I can understand that, Mrs Carmichael, but in an investigation such as we're conducting, we need answers to awkward questions.'

Laura met Fitzjohn's intense gaze. 'Very well, if you must know, it's because she was always far too familiar with my husband. Not that Richard encouraged her, you understand. I think he was oblivious to her attentions. Nevertheless, it irritated me no end.'

In the early evening, with the city buildings still generating the day's heat, Fitzjohn and Williams returned to Day Street Station where Fitzjohn found Betts writing up his notes in the Incident Room. 'How did you get on with Newberry's alibi?' he asked, taking his suit coat off and hanging it on the back of one of the chairs.

'I found discrepancies in the times that he gave us as to when he saw his prospective clients for quotes, sir.' Betts closed his notebook and sat back in his chair. 'He only saw one of the clients listed, and that person said Newberry arrived an hour earlier than scheduled. The other two clients said he didn't turn up at all and didn't telephone to cancel.'

'So where was he, and why lie to us when it's so easy for us to find out? We'll speak to him again, Betts.'

'What did Laura Carmichael have to say, sir?' asked Betts as they left the room.

'She doesn't like Amanda Marsh.' Fitzjohn's eyebrows lifted before he recounted his interview with Laura Carmichael. 'So, not only do we have Sebastian Newberry establishing a motive for Amanda Marsh to kill Rachael Carmichael, we also have Mrs Carmichael stating that Marsh was far too familiar when speaking to her husband. Arrange for her to be brought in next for questioning, Betts. I'd like to know why she, too, denied knowing Peter Van Goren.'

With the rumble of thunder and lightning flashing intermittently in the night sky, Fitzjohn stopped at the front gate to collect the mail before opening the door into his sandstone cottage. The aroma of food met his senses when he stepped inside, and although pleased at the prospect of a fine hot meal, he wondered what price he might have to pay.

'Meg? How was your stay at Sophie's?' he called out, with a hint of hesitancy.

When no reply came, he placed his briefcase down and walked through to the kitchen where he found the table set for dinner, but the room empty. Seeing the back door wide open, he stepped outside onto the porch and peered into the darkened garden. Just visible at the fence bordering Rhonda Butler's property stood Meg, in her hands a tape measure. Curious, he made his way between the flower beds. 'Meg, what are you doing?' As he spoke the metal tape measure screeched and fell to the ground as it retracted.

'*Alistair!* You scared me to death. I didn't expect you home yet.'

'What are you doing?' repeated Fitzjohn.

'I'm making sure my measurements are correct.' Meg picked up the tape measure and put it into her apron pocket.

'Measurements for what?'

'For the trees,' she replied as she stood back and surveyed the fence line. 'It seems I was correct in the first place.' She turned, gave a quick smile, and started toward the house.

'Will you tell me what's going on?' asked Fitzjohn. Meg continued on with Fitzjohn at her heels. 'Meg?'

'It's all because of the letter you received from the Council today, Alistair. Hand delivered I might add.' Meg pointed to an A4 sheet of paper, magnetized to the fridge door. 'I don't know where you keep such correspondence, so I thought that that was as good a place as any.'

Fitzjohn whipped the letter from the fridge and began to read.

'I do apologise for opening your mail,' Meg went on. 'But when I returned from Sophie's this morning and was confronted by that man from the Council, I knew I had to open it. And I'm so glad I did because I've been able to fix the problem before it turns into some kind of disaster.'

Ignoring his sister's diatribe, Fitzjohn ran his eyes over the letter. 'The Council have investigated Rhonda Butler's claim and agree that the glass structure, meaning my greenhouse, is a hindrance to Mrs Butler's ability to live comfortably within her home. It instructs me to dismantle the said structure within the week.' Fitzjohn's face reddened. 'I haven't time to deal with this now, but when I do, the Council's going to get an earful from me. Dismantling my greenhouse be damned,' he said, crumpling the letter into a ball, and throwing it onto the kitchen table before reaching for the bottle of Glenfiddich. 'Want one?' he asked as he poured himself a glass. Meg shook her head.

'You don't have to worry, Alistair. It won't come to that. I have everything in hand.'

'Oh?' Fitzjohn sipped his whisky and eyed his sister. 'What do you have in hand?'

'I have six fully grown murraya trees being delivered first thing tomorrow morning. They're fully mature at eight feet tall and planted close together, will form a perfect screen along the fence line between you and the dragon lady.'

Fitzjohn choked on his whisky. 'Is that what you were doing out there in the dark with that tape measure? Measuring for six trees?'

'Yes. I told you, Alistair. I wanted to make sure my measurements are correct before the trees arrive.' Meg patted Fitzjohn's back. 'Don't worry, dear, you can continue with your police business in the knowledge that I'm in full control. There's no way Mrs Butler will be able to complain again about the reflection of the greenhouse glass shining through her kitchen window.'

Fitzjohn gulped the last of his whisky. 'How much is all this going to cost me?' he asked, pouring himself another drink.

'Just over two thousand dollars.' Fitzjohn choked again. 'A small amount to pay when you consider the alternative.' Meg eyed Fitzjohn's glass. 'I don't think it's a good thing to have too many of those, Alistair. It'll spoil your dinner.'

'It doesn't matter,' replied Fitzjohn, gasping for breath. 'I doubt I could eat a thing.'

Ben paced the floor outside the Intensive Care Unit, the doctor's words reverberating in his head. "We plan to stop Emma's medication this morning, Mr Carmichael. Hopefully, she will start to come out of the coma but as I said to you earlier, there are no guarantees."

'Ben?' Jolted from his thoughts, Ben turned to see Joanna. 'How's Em? Any news?'

'Yes. The doctors have stopped her medication. Now all we can do is pray that she wakes up.'

Joanna put her hand on her brother's forearm. 'So, it's far from over.' Ben did not reply. 'You look so tired. Why don't you go home and get some rest? I'll stay here and I'll phone if there's any news.'

'I can't. I have to stay until I know she's going to be all right.'

It was in the early hours of the following morning as Ben sat vigil at Emma's bedside that he noticed her eyes flutter. But did they? He sat forward in his chair, unsure. 'Emma? Can you hear me?' Hearing his voice in the quietude of the ICU, one of the nursing staff joined him at Emma's bedside. 'I think she's waking up,' he said.

'There is a change in her pulse and respiratory rate, Mr Carmichael, so I think she's becoming aware of her surroundings.' The nurse smiled. 'It's a good sign, but it might take a few more hours before she's fully lucid. Also, be aware that her vision will probably be a little blurred, so she may not be able to see you right away.'

As the hours passed, Ben slumped down in his chair until a whisper roused him. 'Ben?'

Ben jumped. '*Emma!* You're awake. Thank God!'

'Where am I?'

'In the ICU at North Shore Hospital.'

'How long..?'

'Four or five days. I'm not sure. Just rest, Emma.'

'I have to tell you someth...' Emma's eyes closed.

'Emma?' Frantic, Ben looked around as the nurse on duty approached. 'She isn't... Is she?' he asked.

'It's all right, Mr Carmichael. She's still not fully awake.'

Ben collapsed back into his chair and as the hours ticked by, he slept. When he awoke again, he looked up to see Emma's pale blue eyes looking at him and he smiled. 'You're awake. Really awake this time.'

Emma nodded.

In the days that followed, Emma was moved to a room in North Shore Private Hospital where she eventually learned of Richard Carmichael's untimely death and of her own father's inability to make the journey to Australia to see her. At the same time, her ordeal at Ivy Cottage revisited her in fragments, like shattered pieces of glass. They played on her mind by day and plagued her in the hours of darkness as nightmarish taunts.

'I'm losing my mind, Ben. I know I am.' Emma's eyes brimmed with tears. 'My thoughts are all a muddle. I can't think straight. And I see...' Emma stared past Ben as if at some point on the other side of the room. 'There she is again.'

'Who?' Ben held Emma's trembling hands, a disquieted look on his face.

'The person who attacked me. She looks like someone I know but I can't think who.' Emma slumped back into the pillows, beads of perspiration breaking onto her forehead. 'I am going mad. I know I am.'

'No you're not, darling. You've just been through a terrible ordeal and it's going to take time for your thoughts to become clear again. But they will, I promise.'

Emma lay silent for a moment or two before she said, 'She reminds me of that woman who does the catering for your father's company.'

'You mean Amanda Marsh?'

'I don't know her name, but she has short silver grey hair and her eyes...' Emma shuddered. 'Her eyes are cold.'

Ben adjusted the pillows behind Emma's head as her eyelids fluttered and closed in sleep.

⌒ CHAPTER 17 ⌒

Dressed in a dark grey suit and blue striped tie, Fitzjohn adjusted the matching handkerchief in his breast pocket and made his way downstairs. When he reached the front hall, he found the door open and Meg standing outside on the porch. 'I collected the morning paper earlier if that's what you're looking for.'

'I'm not, Alistair. I'm waiting for the trees to arrive.' Meg craned her neck to see along the roadway. 'They should be here by now. I hope they haven't got caught up in the morning traffic.'

Fitzjohn picked up his briefcase from the hall table and with the morning paper under his arm, he joined Meg on the porch.

'You're not leaving yet are you?' she asked. 'You haven't had breakfast and besides, I want you to be here when the truck gets here.'

'I'm sorry, Meg, but I have an early start. Anyway, I'm sure you'll do very well without me here. Just remember to get the company's bank details so that I can pay them on-line.'

'But...'

Fitzjohn gave a wave and closed the front gate behind him before continuing along the footpath. As he turned the corner, a large truck passed by, loaded with trees. With a sigh of relief tinged with guilt at leaving Meg to deal with them alone, he walked on through Birchgrove. It was when he reached his favourite cafe on Rowntree Street that his mobile phone rang.

'Fitzjohn here.'

'What time would you like me to pick you up this morning, sir?' came Betts's voice.

'Whenever you can get here, Betts, but I'm not at home. You'll find me at the Charlotte Cafe.' Fitzjohn settled himself at an outdoor table, opened his newspaper, and sipped his coffee, the guilt he had felt earlier, dissipating as a feeling of calm descended upon him.

———⋙•⋘———

'Morning, sir,' said Betts, taking the opposite seat at the small table. 'This is a nice change,' he continued, looking around. 'Too bad I've already had breakfast.'

'Well, you can join me for coffee,' replied Fitzjohn, taking a large bite of his croissant. 'I felt it necessary to take evasive action this morning. Meg has taken it upon herself to take on not only Rhonda Butler, but also the Leichardt Municipal Council.'

'What's she planning on doing, marching on the council chambers?'

'No, but I wouldn't put it past her.' Fitzjohn recounted the previous evening's events.

'I don't think planting a hedge is going to stop Mrs Butler, sir, because it's not really about the greenhouse. It's about creating as much trouble for you as she can.'

'We know that, Betts, but I don't think Meg sees the bigger picture.'

Fitzjohn walked in the rear entrance of Day Street Police Station to be met by the Duty Officer. 'Mr Carmichael is here to see you, sir. Shall I bring him through?'

'Yes, Sergeant. Show him to my office would you, please? I'll be right there.' Fitzjohn turned to Betts. 'I wonder if he's recalled anything else about the day his mother died.'

'Or it might be about his fiancée, sir.'

'Well, if it is, I hope it's good news.' Fitzjohn continued on to his office to find Ben pacing the floor, the dark shadows under his eyes all too visible.

'Good morning, Mr Carmichael. I take it you have news for me.'

Ben took Fitzjohn's outstretched hand before they sat down. 'I do, Chief Inspector. It's about Emma. I'm happy to say that she's been successfully brought out of the coma and she's making progress, albeit slowly.'

'Well, that is good news,' replied Fitzjohn, smiling. 'I'm glad to hear it. You must be relieved.'

'I am. It's not the only reason I'm here though. You see, I know you'll want to speak to Emma about what happened at Lane's End, but before you do I thought you should know what she's been telling me about the person who attacked her.'

'So, has she remembered all that happened?'

'Not exactly. Her thoughts are disjointed and confused, but she does seem to think that she was attacked by a woman.'

'I see? Is she able to describe this person?'

'Yes, and that's where the confusion comes in.' Ben Carmichael relayed what Emma had told him. 'It's obvious that Emma has Amanda Marsh confused with whoever did attack her, but she is certain what that woman was doing when she arrived at Ivy Cottage. She was tearing up a photograph. I guess the one of my mother that the police found there that day.' Ben shook his head. 'It sounds bizarre, I know, and isn't much to go on.'

'Every piece of information is useful to us, Mr Carmichael. You're aware, of course, that DS Betts and I aren't assigned to Emma's case. DCI Roberts is heading up that investigation so I'll inform him of what you've told me. He'll want to speak to Emma, of course.' Fitzjohn thought for a moment. 'Be there when he does. With what your fiancée has been through, it might be difficult for her to speak of her ordeal to anyone other than yourself.'

Fitzjohn sat back in his chair after Ben Carmichael left the office and pondered their meeting. It was evident that Emma Phillip's ordeal and the death of his father had had a profound effect on the young man. One could see it in his face. Weariness and a deep sadness. But there was something else there too. What was it?

'Sir?' Disturbed from his thoughts, Fitzjohn looked up to see Betts. 'I'll arrange to have Ms Marsh brought in now.'

'Hold on, Betts. I need to speak to you first because I've had second thoughts on the matter.' Fitzjohn recounted his conversation with Ben Carmichael. 'So, no matter how unlikely, the fact that Emma Phillips has named Amanda Marsh as her possible attacker, it means that our investigation now overlaps with DCI Roberts's. Therefore, we'll need to collaborate with him. I'm going to suggest to Roberts that we arrange for a warrant to search Ms Marsh's home and her business premises before we interview her.'

'What, exactly, are we looking for, sir? The Magistrate will want to know.'

'To tell you the truth, I'm not sure.' Fitzjohn frowned. 'Make it photographs of the Carmichael family. Either torn or intact.'

'Very well, sir.'

CHAPTER 18

Fitzjohn and Betts, along with a number of uniformed personnel, arrived at Amanda Marsh's home later that day. They congregated on the small tiled front verandah amid an array of potted plants until the front door opened and Amanda appeared. Dressed casually in a pair of blue jeans and black tank top, she took the cigarette from her lips and gaped at those gathered before her.

'Afternoon, Chief Inspector. Does this mean you have more questions for me or is it an invasion?'

'Good afternoon, Ms Marsh,' said Fitzjohn. 'We have a warrant to search your home.'

'A what! Can I ask what you hope to find?'

Fitzjohn ignored the question and handed the warrant to Amanda. 'I should also inform you that a warrant has been issued to search your business premises. The searches are being conducted simultaneously.'

Amanda ignored Fitzjohn and read the warrant, her free arm wrapped around herself. 'This says you're looking for photographs. What photographs?'

'May we come in?' asked Fitzjohn.

'I don't suppose it's going to do much good to refuse since you've brought reinforcements.' With an indignant air, Amanda stepped aside. The uniformed officers, along with Betts, dispersed into her home, the old wooden floorboards squeaking under their weight.

'Why don't we wait in there whilst my officers conduct their search,' said Fitzjohn, gesturing through an archway into the living room.

Amanda glared at Fitzjohn. 'I'll be complaining to your superior, Chief Inspector.'

'As you wish, Ms Marsh.' Fitzjohn followed Amanda into the room. Ignoring him, she sat on the arm of one of the chairs and put another cigarette to her lips before she exhaled and watched the smoke curl into the air. 'Our search shouldn't take too long,' Fitzjohn continued. His comment met stony silence. Unperturbed, he circled the room, taking in the long coffee table in front of one of the sofas, its surface displaying a pile of House & Garden magazines and in the centre, a large white candle. Skirting the table, he ran an eye along the titles that filled the bookshelves on either side of the fireplace, taking particular interest in a collection on gardening. One well-thumbed book in this series he pulled out and examined. 'You have a fine library on a variety of subjects, Ms Marsh. It'd be the envy of any librarian.' Amanda remained silent.

When Betts reappeared some time later, Fitzjohn joined him in the hallway. 'We've found several photographs, sir. All of Richard Carmichael. Those featuring other people as well, have been mutilated. We also found this in the laundry basket.' Betts looked to one of the uniformed officers who held open a large plastic grocery bag. Fitzjohn peered inside at a bloodied garment.

'That looks troubling. Get forensics in, Betts, and have it sent to the lab. Ms Marsh will accompany us to the station for questioning.'

'Yes, sir.'

———

Fitzjohn sat in his office mulling over the significance of the garment that had been found in Amanda Marsh's home. He looked up when the door opened and Betts walked in. 'Any news on that clothing, Betts?'

'Yes, sir. It's part of Ms Marsh's caterer's uniform. Her name is printed on the inside label so it doesn't belong to Emma Phillips, but the blood does.'

Fitzjohn sat back in his chair. 'Presumably it was what Amanda Marsh was wearing when she attacked Emma Phillips at Ivy Cottage. We'll take it in with us when we question her.'

———

Accompanied by a solicitor, Amanda sat in silence as the door to the interview room opened and Fitzjohn and Betts walked in. Fitzjohn placed his papers and a large plastic bag containing the garment on the table and sat down. Once preliminaries had been completed, he said, 'Ms Marsh, you've been brought in for questioning because a certain item of clothing, found in your home, links you to an attack that was perpetrated against Emma Phillips at Lane's End on Saturday, March 26th. Can you tell us where you were on that day?'

'As I told you before, Chief Inspector, I spent the day at my office.'

'Are you sure about that?'

'Yes, quite sure.'

'Very well, in that case, do you recognise this garment?' As he spoke, Fitzjohn laid out the plastic bag containing the blood splattered uniform.

'You know it's mine. You took it from my home,' replied Amanda with a sneer.

'How did it get splattered with blood?' asked Fitzjohn.

'It happened last week at work when I was cutting up some red meat. I took it home to wash.'

'The blood on this garment isn't animal blood, Ms Marsh.' Amanda looked blankly at Fitzjohn. 'It's Emma Phillips's blood. A young woman who was attacked at Lane's End on March 26th.' Fitzjohn's eyes locked onto Amanda's. 'How did Emma Phillips's blood get onto your uniform if you weren't at Lane's End?'

'It isn't her blood. How could it be? That's a ridiculous suggestion.' Amanda Marsh avoided looking at Fitzjohn as she shifted in her chair.

Fitzjohn sighed. 'Very well, we'll leave the garment for the time being. Let's talk about where you were on Saturday, March 26th. If you weren't at Lane's End, where were you?'

'I've already told you. I spent the day at work.'

'But that's not the case,' replied Fitzjohn. 'We've checked. None of your staff saw you that day.' Amanda did not reply. 'Well? Where were you?'

'All right, I was at Lane's End.'

'Why?'

Amanda glared at Fitzjohn.

'Why were you there, Ms Marsh? he asked again.

'Because... I like to go there sometimes. Just to look at the place.' Amanda smiled to herself as if in reflection. 'I was happy there. But this time...' The smile left Amanda's face.

'This time what?' asked Fitzjohn.

'This time Rachael was there.'

'*Rachael*? But Rachael Carmichael died in 1983.'

'I know that, but she was there, just the same. It made me angry because she spoilt my visit that day, just like she'd always spoilt things.'

Fitzjohn glanced at Betts before he continued. 'What had Rachael always spoilt?'

'My life. Richard's life. Richard deserved someone better than that trollop.' Amanda looked around distractedly. 'I need a cigarette. Can I smoke in here?'

'There's no smoking allowed in the building,' replied Fitzjohn. 'You say that Richard deserved someone better than Rachael. Do you mean someone like yourself?'

'Yes. I loved Richard. Rachael didn't. She just used him. Married him for his money and kept Sebastian Newberry on a leash. I could never understand why Sebastian put up with her antics. They argued whenever they were together anyway.'

'Oh? What did they argue about?' asked Fitzjohn, his interest growing.

'It was always about the same thing. Sebastian wanted Rachael to leave Richard and go and live with him in Paris. She refused, of course. After all, she had the best of both worlds. Until Sebastian killed her, that is.'

'What makes you so sure?' asked Fitzjohn.

'Who else would it be?'

'What about the gardener, Henry Beaumont?'

'Mmm. The police thought it was Henry, but it wasn't. He had no reason to kill Rachael. He would have been aware that the only reason Richard kept Lane's End was because of her. She loved the place. Without her, Richard would have sold Lane's End and Henry would have been out of a job.' Amanda shook her head. 'No. Sebastian did it. He killed that man who died at the Observatory last Friday night too.'

'He did? But what reason would he have?'

'Because, Chief Inspector, Peter Van Goren was really Henry Beaumont, and I believe he'd witnessed Sebastian pushing Rachael off that cliff all those years ago.'

Fitzjohn left the interview room as Betts read Amanda Marsh her rights over the attack on Emma Phillips.

'Now I've heard it all,' said Betts as he walked into Fitzjohn's office and slumped down into a chair. 'Telling us she'd lashed out at an apparition. The woman must be unbalanced to think we're going to believe such rubbish.'

'She may well be unbalanced,' replied Fitzjohn. 'Or faking it. Whatever the case, it's obvious she attacked Emma Phillips whether she believed her to be Rachael Carmichael or not. And as far as her accusation against Newberry goes... well, it sounds plausible, but is it true? Did he push Rachael off that cliff?' Fitzjohn pushed his pen from end to end before he threw it down. 'I hate to say it, Betts, but the deeper we get into this case the less we can be sure of. We're going to have to dig deeper. Let's talk to the Hunts again. I want to know why they agreed to Newberry's request that they deny knowing Peter Van Goren. Arrange for them to be brought in for questioning first thing in the morning. Oh, and we'll speak to them separately.'

'Yes, sir.' Betts got to his feet. 'Can I give you a lift home?'

'Thanks, but you go on. I'll get a cab. I want to speak to Chief Superintendent Grieg before I leave this evening.'

Fitzjohn walked into Grieg's office some time later. He found the Chief Superintendent standing behind his desk placing papers into his briefcase. Grieg looked up when Fitzjohn appeared. 'Yes? What is it?'

'I need to speak to you, sir.'

'It'll have to wait till the morning,' replied Grieg as he closed his briefcase. 'I've got an appointment and I'm already late.'

'I'm afraid this can't wait,' replied Fitzjohn.

Grieg's face reddened, his annoyance evident. 'All right, be quick. What is it?' he barked, sitting down heavily in his chair.

'It's in regards to Detective Senior Constable Williams, sir.'

'Oh?' Grieg's brow furrowed. 'What about him?'

'He's expressed a wish to return to Kings Cross Station.'

'Well, that's not possible. I need him here. And why did he go to you with this request? I'm the one around here who says where and when staff get transferred.'

'He came to me because I'm part of the reason he wants a transfer,' replied Fitzjohn.

'You mean you two don't get on?'

'On the contrary, Williams and I get along very well. He's a fine police officer and can look forward to a successful career, but not if you continue to use him as a mole.'

'*I beg your pardon?*'

'You heard me,' replied Fitzjohn. 'I'm well aware you transferred Williams to Kings Cross Station last autumn so he could report back to you about the Michael Rossi case, and I'm also aware that he's now back here at Day Street for the same reason. To spy on me and report to you.'

'How *dare* you accuse me?' screamed Grieg.

Fitzjohn bent low over Grieg's desk, his right hand resting on the briefcase, his eyes boring into the Chief Superintendent's pudgy face. 'I dare, Chief Superintendent, because it's true, and if you don't stop, the police force will lose a fine young man in Williams. I'm not going to let that happen.'

'I'll have you for this, Fitzjohn. You can kiss your career goodbye right now.'

'If I go, you'll go with me.' Fitzjohn straightened up. 'I'll make sure of it.'

'*Get out! Now!*'

Fitzjohn turned and left Grieg's office. Outside, he adjusted his tie, straightened his suit coat and smiled a wry smile. 'That felt *so* good.'

☞ CHAPTER 19 ☜

E arly the next morning, Fitzjohn stood at the front gate and waved to Meg as her taxi left for the airport. At the same time, he breathed a sigh of relief. 'I love you, sister dear, but in small doses,' he said quietly to himself before turning and walking along the side of the house to the back garden. Once there, he stopped. The garden, usually full of morning sun at this hour, lay in shadow, the grass still wet with dew and the chatter of birds in the bird bath, absent. Fitzjohn lifted his gaze to the source of the shade. The row of murraya trees that, now planted, formed a thick hedge along the fence line. What a fool I've been! So distracted with thoughts of my investigation I gave no attention to the effect that hedge would have on the rest of the garden. Fitzjohn shook his head and continued on with a determined gait to the greenhouse. There too shadows lingered, the air cold and uninviting. It was then he noticed Betts in the garden, his eyes glued to the hedge. Fitzjohn left the greenhouse and joined him.

'So, this is the hedge, sir. It's certainly changed things.'

'And not for the better,' replied Fitzjohn.

'You could always trim it.'

'If I do that, I'll be back where I started. At least this way Rhonda Butler can't complain about the greenhouse glass reflecting the sun into her kitchen.'

'That's true, but I wouldn't put it past her to find something else to grumble to the Council about, sir. As I said yesterday, I think she lives to annoy you.'

'I'm sure she does, Betts.' Fitzjohn chuckled. 'Well, I suppose if for nothing else, I give the woman a reason to get up in the morning.'

'Uncle Alistair.' Fitzjohn and Betts turned to see Sophie, her dark shoulder length hair framing a bright smiling face. 'Hello, Martin. Lovely to see you again. I take it you got your sweater back.'

'Yes. I did,' replied Betts, mesmerized by Sophie's deep blue eyes.

Fitzjohn cleared his throat. 'If you're here to see your mother off, I'm afraid you've just missed her, Sophie,' he said, breaking the spell.

'Oh, that's a shame. Well, not to worry. I'll call her later.' It was then that Sophie looked around. 'What's changed? Something has.' Fitzjohn pointed to the hedge. 'Oh.' Sophie grimaced. 'Well, I hate to say this, Uncle Alistair, but that hedge is spoiling the ambience of your garden. Why on earth did you put it in?'

'It's a long story,' chimed Fitzjohn and Betts.

'I'll bet it has something to do with my mother. She mentioned that she'd solved your neighbour problem.'

'She was only trying to help.' Fitzjohn looked at his watch. 'Come on, Betts. We've got the Hunts to interview.'

'Yes, sir.' Betts turned to Sophie. 'Can we drop you in the city, Soph?'

'Yes, that would be great. Thanks'

Fitzjohn glared at Betts.

'Soph? You call my niece Soph?'

'It's a term of endearment, sir,' replied Betts, striding into the station after Fitzjohn.

'Well, all I can say is, you'd better start trying to endear yourself to me if you know what's good for you.' A half smile crossed Fitzjohn's face as he continued on to his office. 'We've got work to do. Is everything set up for our interviews with the Hunts?'

'Yes, sir.'

'Good. We'll do them simultaneously. You can take Emerson while I talk to Mrs Hunt.'

A short time later, Fitzjohn and Williams walked into the interview room to find Theodora sitting alone. She jumped when the door opened and the two officers appeared.

'Good morning, Mrs Hunt,' said Fitzjohn, taking his place in the chair across from her. 'Thank you for coming in.' Fitzjohn looked at the empty chair next to her. 'Don't you wish to have counsel?' Theodora gave Fitzjohn a blank look. 'I assume you were told that your solicitor could be present.'

'Yes, I was told, but I didn't think I'd need one.'

Fitzjohn noted the nervous inflection in her voice. 'Very well. If you change your mind during the course of our interview, you will let us know, won't you?'

Theodora smiled, her eyes darting to Williams who was preparing the recording machine. 'Is this going to be recorded?' she asked.

'That's normal procedure, Mrs Hunt,' replied Fitzjohn. 'All you need to do is introduce yourself prior to me asking you questions.' Theodora Hunt nodded and cleared her throat.

Williams switched the device on and stated the date and time. After introductions were made, Fitzjohn started the interview.

'Mrs Hunt, when we spoke previously, you told us of Richard Carmichael's first wife, Rachael. Can you tell us how they met?'

'I thought you'd want to ask me more questions about the death at the Observatory. Why are you so interested in Rachael?'

'If you'll just answer the question, Mrs Hunt.'

'Oh. All right.' Theodora glanced again at the recording machine and cleared her throat for a second time before her eyes settled on Fitzjohn. 'Richard met Rachael through Sebastian,' she said, haltingly.

'And?' Fitzjohn waited for Theodora to continue. 'There's no reason to be nervous, Mrs Hunt.'

'I know. I'm sorry. I'll try again. As I said, they met through Sebastian. At the time, he and Rachael were going

out together, but the day he introduced her to his brother...
well, it was obvious that Sebastian found himself on the
outer. I felt a bit sorry for him really. It can't have been easy
since Rachael married Richard within a year of their meeting. Not to mention the fact that Sebastian was best man at
the wedding! He never said anything, of course, but I'm sure
he was devastated.'

'Did Rachael and Sebastian remain on friendly terms?'

'On the surface they did. They had to, but I always felt an
undercurrent between them. After all, it was a bitter pill for
Sebastian to swallow watching the woman he loved married
to his brother. I suppose he was torn because he and Richard
had always been so close. He wouldn't have wanted to hurt
Richard.' Theodora paused. 'Rachael, on the other hand, had
the best of it. Married to Richard, who could provide her
with everything she wanted, and the attentions of Sebastian
with whom she had so much in common. It eventually got to
Sebastian though.'

'How do you know that?' asked Fitzjohn with interest.

'Because I heard them arguing on more than one occasion.
Sebastian wanted Rachael to go with him to Paris! I wasn't
the only one who'd heard them arguing either. Amanda
Marsh told me she'd overheard them too.'

'Ms Marsh told you that?' asked Fitzjohn.

'Yes. In a way, I think it amused her because I don't think
she liked Rachael very much.'

'Oh? What makes you think that, Mrs Hunt?'

'Because she used to criticise Rachael in a subtle kind of
way whenever the opportunity arose. And, of course, she
never stopped talking about Richard. It was obvious she was

besotted with the man.' Theodora lifted her eyebrow. 'Not the sort of woman you want as your housekeeper. If you want to keep your husband, that is. She was absolutely crushed when Richard let her go after Rachael's death. I think she thought she and Richard and the children would all live, happily ever after, together in Mosman.' Theodora chuckled to herself. 'It didn't work out quite the way she expected.'

'You mentioned the last time we spoke that the Carmichaels had another employee at that time. A gardener.'

'Yes,' replied Theodora, guardedly.

'Do you remember his name?' Theodora's eyes darted to the recording device yet again. 'Well?'

'It was Henry. Henry Beaumont.'

'And?' Fitzjohn waited for Theodora to continue. 'Can you tell us anything else about Mr Beaumont?'

'He was French,' said Theodora at last, turning the ring on her right hand. 'In fact, meeting Henry and listening to his tales about Paris is what eventually gave me the idea to open *"Fabrique en France"*.'

'I see. So you spent quite a bit of time talking to Henry, did you?'

'Only when Emerson and I visited Lane's End.'

'What sort of person was he?' continued Fitzjohn.

'He was very nice. Always kept the gardens at Lane's End beautifully.'

'Did he live at Lane's End?'

'Yes, in a small dwelling behind the house.'

'You say he was French. Do you know how he came to be employed by the Carmichaels?'

'I have no idea. I suppose they advertised in the local newspaper.'

'Did he get on well with Rachael do you think?'

'He seemed to. I doubt she had much to do with him. She was always so taken up with her painting whenever she was at Lane's End.'

'Very well.' Fitzjohn looked down at the papers on the table in front of him. 'Let's move on then to the man who died at the Observatory. Peter Van Goren. Previously, you said that you and he talked together early on in the evening. You also said that you'd never met him before. Is that correct?'

'Er... yes. That's right.'

'Are you quite sure about that?' When Theodora did not reply, Fitzjohn continued. 'I should remind you, Mrs Hunt that we're conducting a murder investigation, and withholding information is an offence under the Crimes Act.' Theodora's cheeks reddened. 'Would you like me to repeat the question?' Theodora shifted in her chair. 'Had you met Peter Van Goren prior to the function held at the Observatory on March 12th?'

'No. I don't think so.'

'Was there nothing about the man that was familiar to you?'

'No. Nothing.'

'Not even the fact that he walked with a limp and used a cane. Henry Beaumont walked with a limp and used a cane too, didn't he?'

'I really can't remember. It was a long time ago.'

'Are you sure you didn't know Peter Van Goren, Mrs Hunt, because we're led to believe that each of you present at the Observatory last Friday night, agreed to deny knowing him.'

Theodora gasped. 'Where did you hear that?'

'Is it correct?'

'It was Sebastian. He made Emerson and me agree,' blurted Theodora.

'Did he? Or did you and your husband have your own reasons for denying that you knew Henry Beaumont, alias Peter Van Goren?' Theodora fidgeted again with her ring. 'Why did you lie to us, Mrs Hunt?'

'Because... I thought it would all come out.'

'What would come out?'

'What happened after Rachael died?'

'And what did happen?' asked Fitzjohn.

'Why don't you ask Emerson?'

'Because I'm asking you, Mrs Hunt,' replied Fitzjohn, his intense gaze fixed on Theodora. 'I'll repeat the question. What had you done to make you lie to the police?'

Theodora sank back in her chair and said in all but a whisper, 'We helped Henry hide from the police.'

Fitzjohn's brow furrowed as he looked at Theodora in disbelief. 'I see. Well, in that case, you'd better tell us how your involvement came about from the beginning.'

Theodora bit her lip. 'It began the day that Rachael died. I got a phone call from Henry. He was calling from a public phone in Newport. He was frantic, poor man. He said that Rachael had fallen from the cliff that afternoon and that he would be blamed so he'd packed his bags and left Lane's End.'

'Why did he think he'd be blamed?' asked Fitzjohn.

'Because he saw what happened between Rachael and the other person involved. He told me that that other person threatened to expose him if he stuck around.'

'Expose him for what? What had Henry Beaumont done?'

Theodora hesitated. 'He was an illegal immigrant.'

'Ah. I see,' said Fitzjohn. 'So, damned if he stayed at Lane's End once the police arrived, and certainly damned if he left.' Theodora nodded. 'Did he tell you who this other person was and exactly what had happened?'

'No. He refused to. He thought it would be dangerous for Emerson and me to know. In a way I wish he had told us because I've always wondered. After all, it could only have been one of two people. Sebastian or Amanda Marsh.'

Fitzjohn ignored the assumption and said, 'What exactly did you do when Henry rang you, Mrs Hunt?'

'I panicked. I didn't know what to do, so I told him to wait where he was and I'd come and pick him up.' Theodora swallowed hard. 'I took him home to our house in Seaforth. When Emerson got home that night he had a *fit*. He told me he was going to telephone the police. I begged him not to and finally, he came around. After all, he'd always liked Henry.'

'So, you and Mr Hunt hid Henry Beaumont from the police. A serious matter in itself, Mrs Hunt, but you also did it in the knowledge that Mr Beaumont was an illegal immigrant.'

'I know.' Theodora's large blue eyes stared at Fitzjohn. 'At the time, Emerson told me we could both end up in gaol. Perish the thought. It couldn't still happen now, could it?'

'That depends. How long did you give Henry Beaumont sanctuary?'

'I'm not sure. A matter of weeks. Maybe six. Until the police search had ended, and things quietened down. In the meantime, Emerson helped him make plans to re-establish himself. A new name... he even lent him money to start a business.'

'Did you both keep in touch with Henry Beaumont over the years?'

'No. Henry only contacted Emerson once, and that was to repay the loan. We didn't see him again until that night at the Observatory. You could have knocked me over with a feather.'

'Did Peter Van Goren... Henry Beaumont, I should say, tell you why he was there that night?'

'Yes. He said he'd come to speak to Richard about what he'd witnessed the day that Rachael died. Goodness knows why he chose that particular time and place.'

'Previously, you told us that Richard Carmichael and Peter Van Goren argued when they spoke.'

'Yes. Obviously Richard didn't take the news well.'

'Did you speak to Peter Van Goren again that evening?'

'No.'

———— ✦ ————

Fitzjohn and Williams made their way from the interview room a short time later. On the way, they were joined in the hallway by Betts. Fitzjohn recounted his interview with Theodora Hunt.

'Mr Hunt's story matches his wife's,' said Betts. 'He admits to giving Henry Beaumont refuge in his home at the time the police were searching for him and with full knowledge that he was an illegal immigrant.'

'A damning admission,' said Fitzjohn, entering his office. He gestured to the chairs in front of his desk and Betts and Williams sat down. 'Even so, we need to go through everything again because even though we've gathered all this information, we still don't know who killed Van Goren.' Betts groaned. 'It's either that or admit failure,' continued Fitzjohn.

'We can't do that.' Betts opened his notebook. 'Okay. We've established a link between Peter Van Goren, alias Henry Beaumont, and the Carmichael family. In so doing, it appears likely that whoever killed our victim also killed Rachael. At the time of Rachael's death, and other than the two children, there were only three people at Lane's End. Rachael's brother-in-law, Sebastian Newberry, the housekeeper, Amanda Marsh, and the gardener, Henry Beaumont. We could discount Beaumont as there's a possibility he was framed because of his illegal immigrant status.'

'So that leaves Newberry and Marsh,' said Fitzjohn. 'Both certainly had the opportunity. Amanda Marsh admits that she took lunch to Rachael at mid-day and Sebastian Newberry admits seeking Rachael out as soon as he arrived at Lane's End at one-thirty.'

'And they both had a motive,' put in Betts. 'Newberry, Theodora and Laura Carmichael all paint a picture of Amanda Marsh that suggests she was in love with Richard Carmichael, whereas Amanda Marsh and Theodora Hunt portray Newberry as desperate to have Rachael leave her husband and return to him.'

'Which means that either of them could have pushed Rachael off that cliff,' said Fitzjohn. 'But which one?'

'What about Amanda Marsh's attack on Emma Phillips, sir?' asked Williams. 'In her delusional state, she thought the young woman was Rachael Carmichael come back from the dead, didn't she? It seems a bit telling.'

'That's true, Williams, and she had every opportunity, as well as a motive, to kill Peter Van Goren.' Fitzjohn glanced at the darkened office window. 'It's been a long day, gentlemen, and I think it might benefit us to think on all this overnight. We'll talk again in the morning.' Betts and Williams got up to leave and Fitzjohn started to put his papers into his briefcase. 'Oh. Williams. Before you go.' As Betts disappeared through the open doorway, Williams turned around to face Fitzjohn. 'I've spoken to Chief Superintendent Grieg. Your transfer to Kings Cross Station should come through in a matter of days. If you still wish to go, that is.'

'I don't see any other way, sir.'

'If it's the Chief Superintendent you're worried about, I doubt you'll have any more problems. As I said, I've spoken to him and I can guarantee that there won't be any reprisals on his part.' Fitzjohn paused. 'It's up to you. Of course, there might be other reasons you wish to transfer.'

'There aren't any other reasons, sir. To be honest, I'd sooner stay here at Day Street.'

'Fitzjohn smiled. 'Good man.'

CHAPTER 20

B en turned the key in the lock and opened the front door. The days and nights at Emma's bedside had taken their toll and he promptly slumped down into an armchair in the living room and fell into a deep sleep. Sometime later he awoke to the sound of the doorbell and a voice calling his name.

'Ben? Are you there?'

'Jo?' Ben scrambled to his feet and made his way to the front door to find Joanna.

'Did I wake you? I'm sorry,' she said.

'That's okay. I needed to wake up anyway. Come in.'

Joanna followed Ben into the living room and sat down on the arm of the sofa. 'I called in at the hospital to see Emma and she asked me to pick up a few of her things.'

'Well, that sounds promising. She must be feeling a little better.'

'I believe she is, although, I think she's somewhat confused about what happened to her at Lane's End.'

'Confused and frightened. Did she mention the face that she keeps seeing?'

'No. Is that what's frightening her?' Ben nodded. 'Poor Emma. No wonder she's questioning her sanity. Does she know the face?'

'She described Amanda Marsh when I asked her about it.'

'Amanda? But that doesn't make any sense. What reason would Amanda Marsh have to be at Lane's End?'

'She wouldn't, and Emma knows that, but it's still frightening her. That's why I've stayed with her, especially through the night.'

Joanna looked at her brother's drawn face. 'Well, I'm glad you've come home for an hour or two to rest. You look terrible.'

'Terrible or not, I'm not staying in, Jo. I have to go back to Lane's End.'

'Why?'

'It's hard to explain.'

'Then try. I'd like to know.'

'There's no point.' Ben shook his head. 'It wouldn't make any sense to you.'

'Tell me anyway,' urged Joanna, her curiosity roused.

Ben stared at his sister. 'Okay, but you're going to think I'm losing my mind too.' Ben sighed. 'It all started when I went to the morgue to view Peter Van Goren's body. No, wait a minute, that's not right.' Ben thought for a moment. 'Actually, it began the night you came to tell me that Dad was in the hospital. At the time, you mentioned Mr Van Goren's silver handled cane.

'What began?'

'A terrible feeling gnawing at my insides. It got worse when I went to Lane's End and found Emma at Ivy Cottage. I can't explain it. A sense of dread? Anxiety perhaps?' Ben put his head in his hands. 'I don't know.'

'Then Lane's End is the last place you should be going,' replied Joanna with concern. 'I think you're suffering from stress, and no wonder with Dad passing away, the police investigation, and Emma missing before you eventually found her. Can't you see that?' Joanna shook her head. 'It's all been too much. What you need is rest, and lots of it.'

'It isn't anything to do with being stressed, Joanna.'

'All right. Don't listen to me, but if you insist on going to Lane's End, I'm coming with you. I don't want you going to that place alone. Not again.'

———

Ben pulled the car over onto the shoulder of the deserted lane. 'So, this is it,' said Joanna, wide eyed. 'I've pictured it so many times in my head, but I didn't imagine it would look like a wilderness.' Her gaze went past the gates, rusted and bent on their hinges to the stone wall and beyond into the property. 'It's eerie,' she continued as they walked slowly along the driveway.

'It's been neglected for a long time,' replied Ben as they rounded the bend and the house, struggling to be seen through a tangled mess of vines, came into view.

'Goodness.' Joanna stopped in her tracks. 'I don't know what I expected, but it wasn't this.'

'It wasn't always this way,' said Ben. 'It was once surrounded by a beautiful garden, and that verandah was covered in a flowering vine.'

'It must have been lovely. I wish there were some photos of how it looked.' Joanna walked up onto the verandah and peaked in one of the front windows. 'The furniture's still inside, Ben. Everything's...'

'Everything's as it was the day Dad locked the door on the place thirty years ago.'

'I'd love to go in and look around,' said Joanna, her curiosity growing.

'We can do that, but I want to go down to Ivy Cottage first.'

Joanna sensed her brother's unease. 'Of course. Where is it?' she asked, descending the verandah steps.

'On the other side of the property. Quite a walk, but it shouldn't take too long.' Ben led the way along the side of the house.

'What's that place over there?' asked Joanna as they approached a small dwelling behind the main house.

'It's where the gardener used to live.'

Joanna peered in one of the small windows before standing back and studying the building. 'You know, it was probably very nice at one time, and would be again if it was tidied up a bit and cared for.' As she spoke, Ben continued on towards the tree line. Joanna ran to catch up, picking her way onto the path that led into the bush. 'Oh, this is awful,' she said as her shoes started to soak up the dampness in the undergrowth. 'Do we have to walk through here? Isn't there another way?'

'I'm afraid not. And watch your step. There're vines running everywhere.'

'And spider webs. Ugh! I wonder if Emma walked through here.'

'She'd have had to.'

They continued on, the bird song ending and the sun's rays diminishing the further they went.

'Are you sure we're not lost?' Joanna wiped a spider web from her arm, its substance leaving a sticky residue.

'It's not far now. We're nearly there.' As Ben spoke, the sound of the sea could be heard on the wind, and seconds later they walked out into a clearing overlooking the ocean.

Joanna stopped as the sea breeze hit her face. 'Oh, my goodness. What a beautiful place,' she said, turning a full circle before noticing Ben's contorted expression.

'What is it? *Ben?* Are you all right?'

Ben did not reply, but walked as if in a trance across the clearing to the edge of the cliff. Once there, beads of sweat poured from his brow, and with a sense of déjà vu, his eyes glowered at the rocks below, their surface battered by the ocean swell. Transfixed, he did not feel Joanna grab his trembling arm.

'*Ben!* Come away from the edge. You're making me nervous.'

A child-like scream rang through his head and tears rolled down his face as the full force of what he had seen that day, long ago, played out in his mind.

'*Ben!*' Joanna tried again to pull him back from the edge of the cliff. As she did so, he sank to his knees, his gaze on the frothing rocks below, the expression on his face one of horror.

Unsure what to do, and with her heart pounding, Joanna knelt down next to her brother and waited. Minutes passed before he said, 'I watched her fall.'

'Oh, Ben.' Joanna put her arm around Ben's waist and guided him back up onto the grass verge where he sat with his elbows on his bent knees, his eyes staring out across the sea.

'Henry told me to wait.'

'Henry? Who's Henry?' asked Joanna.

'He was the gardener. Henry Beaumont was his name.' Ben looked at Joanna. 'I'd forgotten we even had a gardener until Theodora mentioned it the other day. Even then I didn't remember anything about him or how he was involved on that day.'

Joanna glared at Ben. 'Are you saying that Henry Beaumont pushed our mother off the cliff?'

'No. She wasn't pushed.'

'You're not saying she *jumped!*' said Joanna, alarmed.

'Not that, either.' With tears brimming his eyelids, the long forgotten memory poured out in a stream of faltering words as he recounted that day. 'I was with Henry that afternoon. Following him around as I always did. When we got to this spot, we saw Mum and Sebastian arguing and struggling over there near the edge of the cliff. Mum broke away from him. When she did, she stumbled. Then she was gone.' A long silence followed before Ben continued. 'Henry left me standing here and ran to help. I guess he could see what could happen, but he didn't get there in time.'

'What about Sebastian?' asked Joanna. 'He must have seen you watching.'

'He was probably too distraught to notice me, and besides, the landscape was different here then. There were a lot more bushes and trees. I doubt he saw me.'

'What happened after that?'

'I'm not sure. There was a lot of shouting and screaming. I don't know who it was. Maybe it was me. All I remember is Henry grabbing me and carrying me back through those trees. He put me down when we got to his stone cottage and he told me to run back to the main house. I never saw him again until...'

'When?'

'The other day. At the morgue in Parramatta.'

Joanna glared at Ben. 'You mean Peter Van Goren was really Henry Beaumont?'

'Yes.'

'That must be why he turned up at the cocktail party. And why he asked after you. He must have gone there to tell Dad what happened here that day.' Joanna looked at Ben. 'And someone murdered him. Who?'

CHAPTER 21

'Looks like you have visitors,' said Joanna as she pulled her car over to the curb. 'It's the Chief Inspector and his Sergeant. You'll be able to tell them what you've remembered.' Ben climbed out of the car and followed by Joanna, made his way through the garden to where the two officers stood talking.

'Ah, Mr Carmichael. Just the man,' said Fitzjohn, turning around. 'We have news.'

'I have some too, Chief Inspector,' replied Ben, unlocking the front door. 'Joanna and I have just come back from Lane's End.' Ben ushered the two police officers into the living room.

'Did you have a particular reason for going there?' asked Fitzjohn as they sat down.

'I did, although it's difficult to describe. You see, since hearing about Peter Van Goren's death and viewing his body at the morgue, I've been getting what I can only describe as flashbacks. Sounds crazy, I know, but that's why I decided to go back to Lane's End today. I'm glad I did because while we were there, it all came back to me. What happened the day our mother died.' Ben recounted what his mind had finally released.

'So your mother's death was an accident, after all,' said Fitzjohn.

'Yes, although it probably wouldn't have happened if she hadn't struggled away from Sebastian.' Ben paused. 'Theodora Hunt mentioned to me the other day that the gardener had left Lane's End that day and he became a hunted man.' Ben shook his head. 'I can't think why he'd do that when all he'd done is try to help. I guess we'll never know.'

'I believe we do know, Mr Carmichael,' replied Fitzjohn. 'You see, Henry Beaumont was an illegal immigrant. A merchant seaman who jumped ship in Sydney. To stay at Lane's End would have meant being questioned by the police about your mother's death. If that happened, he knew he'd be deported if they found out. And they would have. Of course, his leaving made him look guilty.'

'But why didn't Sebastian tell anyone what had really happened?' asked Ben. 'Why let everyone think that there might have been foul play and that Henry was the likely person?'

'Because if he did that, your father would have learnt the truth. That Sebastian and your mother had argued.'

'Do you know why it was so important to him that Dad didn't find that out? Do you know why they argued, Chief Inspector?'

'Yes,' replied Fitzjohn. 'Apparently, Sebastian wanted your mother to leave your father and go live with him in Paris.' The Chief Inspector recounted what he knew of the circumstances surrounding the relationship between Rachael and Sebastian. 'So, with Henry Beaumont gone and all attention drawn to the possibility that he might have been involved in your mother's death, no one would know about Sebastian's argument with your mother and his relationship with your father could continue.'

'So, when Henry... Peter Van Goren turned up at the Observatory that night and spoke to Dad... Chief Inspector, are you saying that Sebastian was the person who killed Peter Van Goren?'

'At this stage, we're not at liberty to discuss Peter Van Goren's death. However, as I said earlier, we do have news that we can speak of, and that is that Emma was right. It was Amanda Marsh who attacked her at Lane's End.'

'But why?' replied Ben, his face agog. 'And what on earth was she doing at Lane's End?'

'We think Ms Marsh may have been delusional at the time. She thought Emma was your mother, Rachael.'

Joanna grimaced. 'But why would she want to attack our mother?'

Fitzjohn hesitated before he continued. 'Well, on searching Ms Marsh's home, we found a collection of photographs. Some that Amanda Marsh probably took with her when she left your father's employ in 1983, and more recent ones taken at various functions that she'd catered for.' Fitzjohn paused. 'It seems that Ms Marsh loved your father and, with your mother gone, thought she could take her place in the home. By all accounts, she was shocked when your grandmother arrived and your father terminated her employment as his housekeeper. Of course, she did devise a way to keep in contact with him through her catering business. Your step-mother, Laura, has accounted for Amanda Marsh's strange behaviour.'

'As far as Peter Van Goren, alias Henry Beaumont, is concerned, it wasn't until he was told he only had a matter of weeks to live that he decided to tell your father what had happened at Lane's End that day.'

'But it doesn't explain why he left the bulk of his estate to me,' said Ben.

'Ah. For that, we do have a possible reason. We've been able to trace Henry's life back to Paris where he was married to a young woman by the name of Yvette Dupois. They had a child. A son they named Eduard. Of course, Henry spent much of his time at sea and during one of his voyages, his young wife and son perished in a fire in the building where they lived. Eduard was five years old at the time. We think that might have been the reason he jumped ship in Sydney. In his grief, he had nothing to go home to.'

'The poor man,' said Ben. 'Perhaps that's why he was always so kind to me.'

'I'm sure it was, Mr Carmichael.'

'Well, that's just blown our whole case,' said Betts, as he and Fitzjohn drove through the Harbour tunnel on their journey back to Sydney's CBD. 'Rachael's death was accidental after all so when Peter Van Goren told Richard Carmichael the truth about his half-brother being present at the time, it means Newberry had no motive to kill Van Goren.' Betts shrugged. 'What do we do now, sir?'

'We'll go back over everything again. There has to be something we've missed.' Betts groaned. 'In a way, it makes it more intriguing, don't you think?' said Fitzjohn with a wry smile as they emerged from the tunnel. 'We'll start by finding out what Amanda Marsh did for a living before she worked as housekeeper for the Carmichaels.'

'I don't see how that's going to help, sir, since we don't have anyone left with a motive to kill Peter Van Goren.'

'Humour me, Betts, and also find out as much as you can about Richard Carmichael before he went into the real estate business. While you're doing that, I'm going to...' As Fitzjohn spoke, a text message came through on his mobile phone. He looked at the screen and his brow wrinkled.

'A problem, sir?'

'It's the Council. I'm asked to call at their office. Well, it'll have to wait.' Fitzjohn put his phone back into his pocket.

Betts laughed. 'What's Mrs Butler complaining about now? The hedge?'

'Apparently so. Its height is cutting out all light into her kitchen.'

'I don't believe it,' said Betts. 'Is there no end to that woman's complaints?'

'I'm beginning to think not, Betts. Nevertheless, the hedge seems to be causing us both problems and it's my fault. I think I'll do what you suggested, and trim it down to fence height even though I'll be back with the initial greenhouse problem.'

⸻

That afternoon, with a sinking feeling, Fitzjohn stood at his office window looking at the rain soaked buildings and slate grey sky, conceding that his greenhouse would have to go. He sighed. As he did so the door behind him opened and Betts burst into the room, his short, curly, ginger hair damp. 'I wondered if you'd get caught in it,' said Fitzjohn, heading for his desk. 'How did you get on?'

Betts brushed the rain from his suit coat and sat down. 'Not bad, although I can't see how this helps our case. Anyway, for what it's worth, prior to her position of housekeeper to the Carmichaels, Amanda Marsh was enrolled in an undergraduate degree course in Pharmacy at the University of Sydney. It's a four year course which she commenced in 1973 but didn't complete. She left in '74.'

'That's interesting,' said Fitzjohn.

'In that case, this next part will blow your mind. Richard Carmichael was enrolled at the University of Sydney at the same time. Or at least for some of it. He did a Bachelor of Arts degree which is a three year course. He completed it at the end of '73.'

'I wonder if that's where those two met?'

'I'd say there's a good chance,' replied Betts. 'because they were both involved in student union activities.'

'In that case, do a little more digging. See what else you can come up with. After that, we'll pay Newberry another call because I'm sure we'll have more questions to ask him by then.'

'We will? I'm confused, sir. I thought we'd done with Newberry.'

'Not quite, Betts, because there's something not right.'

'There is?'

'Yes.' Fitzjohn paused. 'I'm not sure, but I think it might have something to do with that book.' Betts gave a questioning look that Fitzjohn did not miss. 'When we searched Amanda Marsh's home, there was a book in the bookshelf. Well-thumbed and part of a set of gardening books. The other books in that set didn't appear to have ever been opened.'

'So, what makes this book so special other than it's been read a lot?' asked Betts.

'Because it was a book on weeds, Betts.'

'*Weeds?*'

Fitzjohn and Betts arrived at Sebastian Newberry's Ultra Design showroom to find him unlocking the front door. 'Good morning, Mr Newberry,' said Fitzjohn.

Newberry dropped his hand from the door handle and turned around. 'Oh, no. Not you lot again. Look, I've told you everything I know, believe me.'

'I don't doubt it in the least,' replied Fitzjohn. 'However, there are a few things we'd like to go over.'

Newberry gave a heavy sigh. 'Okay. If we must.' He unlocked the showroom door and shoved it open. 'I hope this isn't going to take too long because I have a busy day ahead. We'll talk in my office.' Fitzjohn glanced at Betts and pursed his lips before stepping inside and following Newberry. In his office, Newberry lifted the window blind and sat down behind his desk. 'Okay, what is it you want to know?'

Fitzjohn tried to settle himself on one of the white moulded plastic chairs in front of Newberry's desk. 'Since we last spoke,' he began. 'a witness has come forward.'

'A witness? To what for heaven's sake?'

'To Rachael Carmichael's death,' replied Fitzjohn.

'There weren't any witnesses.'

'Oh? How do you know if you weren't there, Mr Newberry?'

'Because...' Flustered, Newberry glared at Fitzjohn.

'Because you were there, weren't you?'

Avoiding Fitzjohn's question, Sebastian brushed a piece of lint from his sleeve. 'Who is this so-called witness?'

'We can't say,' replied Fitzjohn. 'What I do want to ask you, though, is what condition Rachael was in when you argued with her that day. You did argue with her. Didn't you?'

'We weren't arguing,' said Sebastian. 'We just had a slight difference of opinion about a private matter, but then something happened and...' Newberry's eyes glistened as he relived the past.

'What happened, Mr Newberry?'

'Rachael began to have trouble breathing. At first I thought she was just hyperventilating because she did have a tendency to be a little highly strung, but when I looked into her eyes, they were dilated. Then she started to shake and I panicked. I didn't know what to do. I tried to get her to sit down on the grass but she pulled away from me... in the direction of the cliff.' Newberry frowned. 'She seemed to be disorientated and she was having trouble walking. I went after her. Tried to grab a hold of her but I was too late.' Tears filled Sebastian's eyes and his voice broke. 'She fell.' Sebastian's tear streaked face looked at the two police officers and silence fell over the room. 'I didn't kill Rachael, Chief Inspector. I loved her.'

Fitzjohn waited for a moment before he continued. 'Do you remember exactly what Rachael was doing when you arrived at Ivy Cottage that afternoon, Mr Newberry?'

'What difference does it make? She's gone. Forever.' Newberry wiped his face with his handkerchief.

'It could make a lot of difference,' replied Fitzjohn.

'I can't see how.'

'Nevertheless. If you can just tell us what you remember.'

'Very well. For a start, she wasn't inside the cottage. She was sitting outside on the grass having her lunch in the sun. She said she'd decided to paint out there because it was such a lovely day.'

'Do you remember what she was eating for lunch?'

Sebastian gave Fitzjohn an enquiring look. 'Some sort of salad, I think. Why?'

'How did she seem to you at the time?'

'A bit tetchy, but that might have been because she wasn't feeling well.'

'Did she tell you she wasn't feeling well?'

'Yes. She said she'd felt fine all morning, but must have been coming down with a virus or something. That's why she finally put her lunch aside.' Sebastian met Fitzjohn's gaze. 'These questions, Chief Inspector. Do you know something I don't?'

'Why did you let the police think that Henry Beaumont had pushed Rachael off that cliff when you knew he hadn't?' continued Fitzjohn, ignoring Sebastian's question.

'Because I didn't want Richard to think I had anything to do with Rachael's death. I knew questions would be asked and I thought it might come out that I'd wanted her to leave Richard and go with me to live in Paris. It's as simple as that.'

'So you concocted a story about searching for her which resulted in her death remaining unsolved. What about Henry Beaumont? Did you encourage him to leave the premises before the police arrived?'

'Well, let's put it this way, I didn't dissuade him. After all, if he'd stayed at Lane's End, the police would have found him to be an illegal immigrant and deported him. At least this way, he was able to stay in the country.'

'What made you think he was an illegal immigrant?' asked Fitzjohn.

'Richard told me. In confidence, of course. He said he'd met Henry in the city one day. Apparently, he'd just been told that his wife and child had died. I don't know the circumstances, but it was enough for Richard to take pity on the man and offer him a job at Lane's End.' Sebastian paused. 'Richard was like that.'

'And when you saw Peter Van Goren at the Observatory that Friday night, did you recognise him immediately as Henry Beaumont?'

'I didn't see him until after he'd spoken to Richard about Rachael's death. But, yes, I did recognise him. And if your next question is, did I kill him, the answer is no. Why would I? He'd told Richard everything so the damage was done.'

———

Fitzjohn and Betts emerged from the air-conditioned comfort of Ultra Design and into the morning's growing heat and humidity. 'I don't know that we can believe Newberry, sir. He makes it sound like there was something wrong with Rachael before she went over that cliff, but if that was the case, it would have shown up in the Coroner's Report.'

'Not necessarily, Betts,' replied Fitzjohn, taking off his suit coat and placing it on the back seat before climbing into the car. 'There might have been something in her system that wouldn't be apparent without further testing. The pathologist would only have done that for a reason. Rachael fell off a cliff and whether she fell or was pushed, their attention was on the fact that she died from the fall. Of course, she might have done so, but I wonder now whether there was something else at play. Newberry said himself that Rachael wasn't feeling well when he arrived. And the symptoms he listed - shortness of breath, eyes dilated, body tremor - sounds to me like she'd been poisoned.'

'But how?' asked Betts, turning the ignition and starting the air conditioning system.

'I don't know, but I have a feeling it has something to do with that book on weeds. We'll question Amanda Marsh again.'

Fitzjohn and Betts sat opposite Amanda and her solicitor in the interview room. 'You've already arrested me. Why have you brought me in here again?' she asked, meeting Fitzjohn's fixed gaze.

'Because we'd like to go over what happened on the day you and Rachael arrived at Lane's End.'

'Not again. I've already told you everything I know.'

'Even so, Ms Marsh, we need to get a few more details. You said that on that day you took Rachael's lunch to her at Ivy Cottage.'

'That's right.'

'What exactly did you prepare for her lunch?'

'Her favourite. A chicken salad.'

'And what went into that salad?'

'The usual things. Chicken, of course, some lettuce, tomato, cucumber, avocado, and mayonnaise.'

'What about parsley?'

'That too.'

'Had you taken all these ingredients with you to Lane's End that morning?'

'Of course. Everything was fresh.'

'Including the parsley?'

'Yes. Including the parsley.' Amanda gave Fitzjohn an indignant look. 'Where's all this leading?'

'It's leading to the fact that after eating the salad you prepared for Rachael, she became ill.'

'Rubbish. How would you know?' Amanda's eyes darted between Fitzjohn and Betts. 'Oh, I see. You've been speaking to Sebastian. Well, he would say that, wouldn't he? Wanting to shift the blame for her death onto me.'

'He doesn't have to shift blame onto anyone, Ms Marsh, because Rachael wasn't pushed over that cliff. She fell because she'd become dizzy and disorientated.' Amanda glared at Fitzjohn. 'What did you put in the salad to make Rachael ill?'

'Just what I told you. Why would I want to harm her?'

'You told us earlier that you were in love with her husband, Richard. That's a good enough reason,' replied Fitzjohn. 'Might I suggest that the parsley you put on Rachael's salad wasn't parsley at all, but hemlock. After all, the hemlock leaf will pass for parsley. Enough not to be questioned, anyway.

You know all about such things, don't you, Ms Marsh? Having been a pharmaceutical student at one time.'

'You can't prove any of this.'

'You're probably right. It could be difficult, but it won't be difficult to prove that you murdered Peter Van Goren, alias Henry Beaumont. He had to die, didn't he? After all, he'd recognised what you'd prepared for Rachael, and approached you before he left Lane's End that day. Of course, there wasn't a thing he could do about it until the day he attended the cocktail party at the Observatory. You knew he was there for one reason, to tell Richard Carmichael what had really happened to Rachael. That's why you made yourself scarce until you had the opportunity to end Van Goren's life.'

Amanda sat back in her chair. 'How do you know all this?'

'I'm a detective, Ms Marsh. I detect.'

~ CHAPTER 23 ~

'Thanks for all your hard work over the past couple of weeks, Betts,' said Fitzjohn as he stood behind his desk and placed his papers into his briefcase. 'It hasn't been an easy case. So much so that for a while there, I thought it might have got the better of us.'

'I still don't understand how you knew Henry Beaumont had spoken to Amanda Marsh before he left Lane's End that day, sir,' said Betts, leaning against the filing cabinet.

'I didn't. I just hoped. If I was right, I thought it'd be enough to throw Ms Marsh off balance. You see, it seemed to me that Henry had been an excellent gardener, so I presumed he knew all about noxious weeds as well as the plants he worked with. I also think he was an astute man and would have noticed that there was something wrong with Rachael, physically, when she pulled away from Sebastian. After all, Ben Carmichael did say that Henry had left him behind and run toward them. Being that sort of person I thought there was every possibility he might just have looked around at the scene after Rachael fell and noticed the half eaten salad. Put two and two together, perhaps. And it seems he did.' Fitzjohn paused. 'There was also the fact that Richard Carmichael became angry about the food presentation during the cocktail party that night and said he was going off to speak to Amanda. From what we'd gleaned about his personality being rather placid, that reaction seemed to me to be out of character. Of course, we now know it wasn't that at all, that actually, he'd just learnt from Van Goren that Amanda had attempted to poison Rachael.' Fitzjohn sighed. 'Makes you wonder whether that knowledge was a catalyst for his eventual heart attack, doesn't it?'

'What do you think about Amanda Marsh, sir? Do you think she's sound, psychologically?'

'That's difficult to say until she's assessed. She might well be sound, in which case she missed her calling because she'd have made a successful career on the stage. I tend to think, however, that that's not the case.'

'So you think she believed that Emma Phillips was Rachael that day at Ivy Cottage.'

'Yes. I do.' Fitzjohn closed his briefcase and shrugged into his suit coat before he took in Betts's smart appearance.

'Going somewhere special this evening, are we?'

'I have a date with a certain young lady, sir.'

Fitzjohn gave Betts a knowing look. 'She wouldn't happen to be my niece by any chance, would she?'

'As a matter of fact...'

'Enjoy your evening, Betts,' Fitzjohn said with a smile as he grabbed his briefcase and disappeared through the doorway.

As night time fell and with an ambulance wailing in the distance, Fitzjohn arrived home that evening to be met by the sweet sound of silence as he stepped inside his Birchgrove cottage. Closing the door behind him, he sighed, happy in the expectation of a peaceful evening tending his orchids but, at the same time, saddened by the fact that this pastime was about to come to an end with the demolition of his greenhouse. He placed his briefcase and the mail on the hall table and, humming to himself, he made his way upstairs. Minutes later, now dressed in an old pair of beige slacks and a T-shirt that had seen better days, he made his way back downstairs, through to the kitchen and out into the back garden. There, he stood for a moment or two on the porch reflecting on the successful outcome of not only his investigation into Peter Van Goren's death, but also that of Rachael Carmichael's. It would, of course, remain to be seen what Grieg's reaction to the solving of the latter would be. Good or bad, however, he decided it was a thought for another day. Rubbing his hands together, he stepped off the porch and headed down the garden path toward the greenhouse, looking sideways at the offending murraya hedge as he did so. It was then he realised that he had a surprisingly clear view into Rhonda Butler's garden. Fitzjohn stopped in his tracks, at the same time, looking down at the debris strewn along the fence line. With the hedge now at fence height, he tentatively peered over to see Rhonda armed with a gas powered hedge trimmer. 'Good evening Mrs Butler. Doing a little night time gardening are we?'

Rhonda squealed. 'It's none of your business what I'm doing, Mr Fitzjohn.'

'It is when it's my hedge you're trimming, madam. Let's say, game, set, match, shall we? In other words, I won't make a complaint to the New South Wales Police Department about you tampering with my property if you withdraw your complaint about my greenhouse to Leichhardt Municipal Council.'

'Don't be ridiculous. The police would never listen to you,' sneered Rhonda.

'Oh, but that's where you're wrong. They'll listen because I'm a policeman. Or had you forgotten? Good evening, Mrs B.' Chuckling to himself and with a spring in his step, Fitzjohn stepped over the debris and made his way into the greenhouse. 'The perfect ending to a perfect day,' he said with a smile.

⌒ CHAPTER 24 ⌒

I n the weeks that followed, Emma returned home, at last free from the nightmares that had haunted her days and nights while she recuperated in the hospital. Joanna and Laura set off on a Mediterranean cruise in an effort to put the past behind them and start again. For Ben, the violence and suffering he had witnessed during his years roaming the world, had finally taken their toll and now, he pondered his future.

'Ben?' Emma walked into the study, the only light that from the desk lamp. She placed a mug of steaming coffee down in front of him, its rich aroma filling the air. 'Making plans for your next assignment?' she asked.

Ben leaned back in his chair and took her hands. 'No, because there's not going to be a next assignment. I resigned this morning.'

'*Resigned?* I don't understand. You're not doing it because of me, are you? I wouldn't want that, Ben.'

'That might be part of it, but not all. You see, I can't do it anymore, Emma. I just can't. I knew that when I was on my way back from Cairo this last time.'

'But what will you do?'

'I'll freelance. I'm not sure in what direction. I'll have to give it some thought but in the meantime, I've been asked to do an exhibition of my work in New York.'

'Oh. Well, that's quite an accolade.' Emma paused. 'How long will you be gone?'

Ben shrugged. 'Could be months.'

Emma slumped down into the chair next to Ben's desk. *'Months?'*

'Yes. These things always take time. There's so much to prepare. And the organisers want the exhibition to run for at least one month, possibly longer depending on how well it's received so...' Emma's blue eyes stared at Ben. 'Of course, after we've finished in New York, I thought we could take a holiday in Europe.'

'We?' A wide smile came to Emma's face and she flung her arms around Ben's neck.

'Of course. Do you think I'd go without you?'

As Ben held Emma in his arms, the doorbell sounded. Ben looked at his watch. 'That'll be Emerson. I asked him to drop by because I've decided to put Lane's End on the market.'

Emma sat back. 'Is that wise? What I mean is. Shouldn't you take some time to think about it first? You don't want to do something you might regret.'

'I have thought and I couldn't come up with a reason to keep the place. It's where my mother died a terrible death, and I can't see you wanting to return. Not after what happened to you there.'

'Amanda Marsh might have attacked me at Lane's End, Ben, but I don't have a problem with the place itself. Why would I? But having said that, I can understand that you might not be able to dispel the ghosts that lurk in your mind.'

Ben sighed. 'You're right, there are ghosts.'

'Then wouldn't it be a good idea not to rush into selling?' Emma asked.

———

When Joanna had returned from the Mediterranean and on the afternoon before Ben and Emma left for New York, Joanna and Ben stood on the edge of the cliff at Lane's End, and in the face of a soft sea breeze, threw the roses they held, one by one, out over the cliff top and into the swirling sea below.

SYDNEY OBSERVATORY

The Sydney Observatory that features in Lane's End was built in 1858 and is located on "Observatory Hill" in the heart of Sydney's CBD. It is the oldest existing observatory in Australia.

During the 19th and early 20th centuries it provided time services for the colony, shipping and navigation, surveying measurement and meteorology recording, as well as observing astronomical events and the stars in the Southern Hemisphere sky. In 1982 Sydney Observatory became part of the Museum of Applied Arts and Sciences.

Sydney Observatory's role today is astronomy education, public telescope viewing and the preservation of astronomical heritage. It houses the oldest refractor transit telescope in Australia, an 1874 29cm lens telescope, and a recently restored 1890s astrographic telescope, as well as contemporary computer-controlled reflector and hydrogen-alpha solar telescopes. Day and night tours by astronomers include a virtual reality 3-D space theatre and Digitalis planetarium, and exhibitions about astronomy, meteorology and the Observatory's history.

http://www.sydneyobservatory.com.au
https://www.facebook.com/sydneyobservatory?fref=ts

THE SILVER CANE

The silver cane that features in Lane's End and appears on the book's cover, was hand-crafted in Italy by Pasotti. Founded in 1956 by Ernesta Pasotti, not only does the company make the most beautiful canes you will ever see, they also produce the most exquisite umbrellas.

When I first started to write Lane's End, I envisaged just such a cane. Oddly enough, on one particular Tuesday in 2013, I found myself in a most fascinating shop bursting with antiques, soft furnishings and products from across the world. I'm a good browser so, of course, I stepped inside. There, leaning against an antique cupboard was the very SILVER CANE I had conjured up in my mind, complete with an eagles head for its handle, and a silver tip at its end. No doubt you know the rest. I bought it!

My sincere thanks goes to Nicola Begotti of Pasotti Ombrelli SRL, for giving me his permission to include the silver cane's image on the cover of Lane's End.

www.pasottiombrelli.com
www.facebook.com/PasottiSince1956

ABOUT THE AUTHOR

Jill Paterson was born in Yorkshire, UK, and grew up in Adelaide, South Australia before spending 11 years in Ontario, Canada. On returning to Australia, she settled in Canberra.

After completing an Arts Degree at the Australian National University, she worked at the Australian National University's School of Law before spending the next 10 years with the Business Council of Australia and the University of New South Wales (ADFA Campus) in the School of Electrical Engineering.

Jill is the author of four published books, The Celtic Dagger, Murder At The Rocks, Once Upon A Lie and Lane's End which are all part of the Fitzjohn Mystery Series. She has also authored two non-fiction books entitled Self Publishing-Pocket Guide and Writing-Painting A Picture With Words.

ALSO BY THIS AUTHOR

The *Celtic* Dagger

University professor Alex Wearing is found murdered in his study by the Post Graduate Co-coordinator, Vera Trenbath, a nosey interfering busybody. Assigned to the case is Detective Chief Inspector Alistair Fitzjohn. Fitzjohn is a detective from the old guard, whose methodical, painstaking methods are viewed by some as archaic. His relentless pursuit for the killer zeros in on Alex's brother, James, as a key suspect in his investigation.

Compelled to clear himself of suspicion, James starts his own investigation and finds himself immersed in a web of intrigue, ultimately uncovering long hidden secrets about his brother's life that could easily be the very reasons he was murdered.

This gripping tale of murder and suspense winds its way through the university's hallowed halls to emerge into the beautiful, yet unpredictable, Blue Mountain region where more challenges and obstacles await James in his quest to clear himself of suspicion and uncover the truth about his brother.

Murder At The Rocks

When Laurence Harford, a prominent businessman and philanthropist is found murdered in the historic Rocks area of Sydney, Detective Chief Inspector Fitzjohn is asked to solve the crime quickly and discreetly. After barely starting his investigation, uncovering a discarded mistress and disgruntled employees, a second killing occurs.

Meanwhile, Laurence's nephew, Nicholas Harford, has his certainties in life shaken when he becomes a suspect in his uncle's death, and receives a mysterious gold locket that starts a chain of events unravelling his family's dark truths.

Once Upon A Lie

Little did, businessman and entrepreneur, Michael Rossi know that the telephone call he answered on that fateful Friday would be the catalyst for his death, and the subsequent recovery of his body from the waters of Sydney Harbour the following morning.

Recalled from leave to take on the case, Detective Chief Inspector Fitzjohn confronts the first of many puzzles; how Rossi spent the unaccountable hours before he died. This leads him on a paper-trail into a tangled web of deception, jealousy and greed that unravels the mystery surrounding Michael's death.

Unaware of her nephew's fate, Esme Timmons retires for the evening, unsuspecting of the events about to unfold; events that will, ultimately, expose a grim lie, buried deep in the past.

The Celtic Dagger, Murder At The Rocks, and *Once Upon A Lie* are available on Amazon. http://www.amazon.com/author/jillpaterson

CONNECT WITH ME ON-LINE

My Blog
http://www.theperfectplot.blogspot.com

Twitter
http://twitter.com/JillPaterson2

Facebook
http://www.facebook.com/jillpaterson.author

Goodreads
http://www.goodreads.com/author/show/4445926.Jill_Paterson

Official Website
http://www.jillpaterson.com

Amazon
http://www.amazon.com/author/jillpaterson